KIRKBRIDE AND COMPANY

KIRKBRIDE AND COMPANY

By

HARRY BLAMIRES

LONDON

S · P · C · K

1959

First published 1959
by S.P.C.K.
Holy Trinity Church
Marylebone Road
London, N.W.1

Made and printed in Great Britain by
William Clowes and Sons, Limited
London and Beccles

All the characters in this book are fictitious.
No reference is intended to any living person.

I

"It's a mystery to me that a daughter of mine should take to a man like Howard Prentice." Mr Lyte's voice was cold, almost harsh. "I'll have another piece of toast, my dear."

"Yes, it's a little surprising." Mrs Lyte's agreement sounded half-hearted. "There's plenty of butter, Tony. I'm sure we can trust Elizabeth."

Mr Lyte pricked up his ears.

"That's the postman, I think. Yes, my dear, as I was saying, I can't understand it at all."

There were others too who found the friendship between Howard Prentice and Elizabeth Lyte hard to understand, and some indeed who found it distressing. Mildred Spruice, for instance. When she first heard about it, she was taken aback. It was not merely that she hated losing Howard to someone else. In a way she was prepared for that and half-expected it. Everyone learns something from experience, and, deep down, Mildred had always reckoned with the fact that a man like Howard, who blows in like a whirlwind, may eventually sidle out like a frightened cat. But nevertheless the abruptness of the change hurt her acutely. For, according to Valerie, this girl Elizabeth Lyte was scarcely more than a schoolgirl—a child with the eyes of a doe and the defences of a shorn lamb. She was pale and prudish, and taught in the Sunday School at All Saints', Nunswood. It was a frightful let-down. Although Mildred had long ago ceased to mistake Howard's bluster for strength and masterfulness, she had hoped he was too big and demanding to start baby-snatching.

She was hurt too that Howard had not come clean; that he had continued to come to see her when it was obviously no more than a matter of keeping up appearances. Hurt that he should have lacked the spirit to make a proper break; that he should have persisted in this phony chivalry of waiting for her to take the initiative.

Mildred was the last person to conceal her annoyance, and when Howard turned up on the Friday night, blazing in with his usual surface froth and chatter, she killed the performance stone dead.

"I can't think why you've troubled to come," she said, her back to him as he settled his great length sprawlingly in an armchair. "How did you manage to tear yourself away?"

"From what?" There was just the faintest hint of a challenge behind the tremor.

Mildred lit a cigarette, and she didn't hurry over it.

"Miss Lyte," she said casually, "the sweet little girl in the front pew."

"Oh, that!"

Howard spoke as though the subject could be dismissed as of no account.

"Yes, that."

2

Hell, thought Howard, she's going to play the frozen martyr. He shifted awkwardly in his chair.

Mildred pulled slowly at her cigarette.

"I can't quite picture you with a girl like that," she said meditatively.

Howard was silent. Totally deflated. This was a situation with which he could not cope. He hadn't the equipment. His sole social technique was that of the steam-roller. Flippant, garrulous, effervescent, he could, on first acquaintance, stampede people into silence if not into admiration. He carried the day, with less assertive souls, by means of a chatty, off-hand *bonhomie* that swept the atmosphere clean of reflection or gravity. That was fine so long as he was advancing and on top. But when the quiet, probing challenge came to check him, he collapsed. He might murmur inwardly, but he didn't know how to defend himself.

Had Mildred sensed this? She knelt down on the hearth-rug, picked up the poker, and gently inserted it into the fire, as though she were testing the consistency of a half-baked cake. Not that the fire needed to be prodded; but it was an expressively ruminative gesture. It was also a calm, unflurried gesture—the gesture of one who was not in the dock. Howard stared at her black hair, not now to savour its sheen, but to regret that he could not read the brain it concealed. Was she annoyed, or merely out to annoy?

"You were always quite good as the blue-eyed boy, Howard, but this kind of thing . . ." The sentence trailed off expressively.

"Which kind of thing?"

"Going through your paces with the local teenagers."

3

Howard decided to assert himself.

"So far you have named one young lady only. And she happens to be the kind of person with whom it would be impossible to go through paces, as you put it."

"You've soon found that out."

He waved his hand in deprecation.

"It's neither here nor there," Mildred said, unconvincingly patting her hair at the back. "But I just wondered why you had troubled to come here to-night."

Howard felt that he was really trapped now. He would have to reply either that he wanted Mildred's company, or that he wanted to make a break. And he was not prepared to risk the immediate results of saying either. So he kept quiet. And Mildred threw her cigarette into the fire, then turned her back on him and leaned against his legs. He was mystified. Was it that she needed him physically even now? Or was she being clever? He was in the disadvantageous position of not being able to see her face. Perhaps that was what she intended.

"Have you seen Conrad lately?"

"Not lately."

"I have."

This was a surprise to Howard. Conrad, Mildred's husband, had left her three years ago. What was in the air?

"Did you have a chat?"

"Yes, a very interesting one."

Mildred seemed to be trying to make it sound enormously significant. Howard, not anxious to prolong hostilities, played up.

"Something special?"

4

"Yes. We're going to get a divorce."

The words seemed to drop, echoing, into a great silent emptiness.

"Oh . . . good." Howard's voice sounded suddenly weak and remote. "You'll be glad of that."

"And you?"

"Why, yes, of course."

"Why 'of course'?"

Howard began to feel hot under the collar. He hedged awkwardly.

"Well, it's right that you should be free, after all that has happened. I'm glad Conrad is being sensible at last."

"You've taken it very well."

Howard stared at the back of Mildred's head. Just how much sarcasm was there in all this? The tone of voice was oddly unexpressive. Seconds passed, while he kept his lips resolutely closed, waiting for the next volley.

"It means I can get married, Howard."

"Eventually." Howard was on guard now and spoke deliberately. "It will be soon enough to think about that when the divorce is through."

Mildred's head fell back on to his knees.

"So you see why I'm interested in little Miss Lyte?"

Howard was beaten by her very proximity and gentleness. No doubt it was all a great pose, but it seemed to strip him bare of coverage, leaving him with no heart for anything except futile evasion.

"Don't be silly, Mildred."

"Oh. Things are as they were, then?"

Howard was conscious of the sweat around his

shoulders. Mildred was still as a statue, and his knee trembled momentarily under her head. He rebelled against its confession in fatuous injured vanity.

"Why not?"

Suddenly she leaped forward, turned, and faced him.

"Don't be so stupid, Howard. You can't marry me."

Howard shrugged his shoulders and grinned superciliously.

"The general view would be that I could scarcely do anything else."

"Well, you can't."

"You seem very sure."

Mildred turned her head away.

"You don't want to," she said.

This came out with a superficial cheerful decisiveness which Howard, unsubtle as he was, quite failed to penetrate. Totally unaware of what Mildred's words were secretly costing her, he received them as a challenge to his own genuineness, the genuineness of his own past. Thus, though he was quite incapable of issuing a direct denial of Mildred's charge, he suddenly felt inexplicably possessive towards her. As if aware of this feeling and anxious to encourage it, Mildred leaned forward against his legs.

"You're a child, Howard. And you're quite hopeless with women."

"Am I?"

She nodded.

"Then there's nothing to worry about, is there?"

This was just a shade too clever. The words carried the implication that Howard was now free to run his own separate course in his own way, clear of guilt or

6

charge. And the nervous little laugh with which he rounded the sentence off brought a quick flush to Mildred's cheeks. She pulled herself back and turned her head. Howard sensed at once that he had hurt her, and his sympathies were touched. He leaned forward.

"I'm sorry," he said gently.

But it was no use. The falsehood cried to heaven and Mildred knew it.

"You're nothing of the kind."

"All right. I'm a liar."

"Yes." Mildred's voice was suddenly quieter. "Or you wouldn't have come here to-night. That's it. I can read you like a book. You're wondering all the time how to get away from me. And for all I care, you can walk straight out."

For all that she was stung, she was only just managing to hold back the tears. But Howard was too preoccupied with his own injured feelings to sense the depth of her distress. To be told that his presence was of so little significance was hardly likely to hearten him. A new note of offence crept into his voice.

"I did think there was more between us than that."

"And that's why you took up with Elizabeth Lyte."

Howard blushed. He was beginning to get himself tied up. He fenced.

"I'm not a brute."

"Not a brute. No. Just an actor. That's what you are. And that's why you came here to-night. You wanted a nice little tragic scene with the little woman at your feet."

"No, Mildred . . ."

7

The deprecatory tone was hollow. And not surprisingly. For momentarily Howard indulged the fraction of a dreadful fear that she might be right. Certainly he wanted something more than casualness or abuse. He was reluctant to see his affair with Mildred lowered retrospectively to the level of a stop-gap liaison. It was neither honest nor dignified to behave as though their coming together had been trivial from first to last. So what? Was he therefore a hypocrite? Was it ignoble to have believed that he and Mildred had grown to mean something to each other? He made another attempt.

"Mildred, it's not like you to be so crude . . ."

But he stopped himself. For suddenly he saw Mildred's eyes and her mouth and her throat. She was all but sobbing aloud. Nervously his hand touched her shoulder; but she shook it off and rose to her feet.

"Go away," she said, in a dreary, dead voice. "Go away."

"I'm astonished that Elizabeth continues to see Howard Prentice," Mr Lyte observed, removing five envelopes from his plate and stuffing them, unexamined, into his pocket. "He's well over thirty, you know."

"I'm sure there's nothing to worry about, dear," his wife replied, in a voice less confident than her words. "It's best not to interfere."

Mr Lyte propped up his morning paper against the tea-pot.

"I hope you're right," he said.

There was an air of restrained elation about the heavy

claret curtains and cream wall-panelling of the Dining-Room in the Royal Hotel. The waiters moved deftly among the tables, their noiseless tread cunningly producing the impression that the floor was more luxuriously carpeted than in fact it was. Pink wall lights multiplied themselves in wall mirrors, proliferating in a milky way, strawberry flavoured, all round the room. The enveloping glow stopped some degrees short of the voluptuous, as befitted the dignity of the Royal, but Elizabeth's pale features were delicately flushed and the wine glasses sang with colour.

Howard was only half contented. True, it was a creditable step to have persuaded Elizabeth to come out with him once more to dinner; yet there was no decisiveness about the situation. He felt like a man short-listed for a promotion. There was a considerable achievement behind him, yet it seemed only to sharpen the contrast between possible failure and possible success in the future. Circumspection was more needful than ever, for at first there was a remoteness in Elizabeth's eyes, as though she were not sure of herself, as though perhaps she feared she ought not to have come. But if she was a little too consciously gracious at the soup stage, she was effortlessly so by the time the sweet was served. And when the two of them eventually moved into the lounge for coffee, Howard thought he saw traces of an Elizabeth much mellower yet.

There, in the lounge, dimly lit, the atmosphere was easier and cosier, and Howard allowed his eyes to wander over Elizabeth with the darting gentleness of a bird exploring a patch of ground. Her wide eyes, her swept-back hair, and her slightly parted lips all seemed

9

to promise an accessibility still to be savoured. But she was wearing black, and this, though it added softness to her white arms and neck, gave also a certain unrelaxing formality to her bearing. She sat now on the edge of her chair, presiding at the coffee table with a gentle, uncommitted dignity which Howard found provocative. He wanted to break through it. A hotel lounge might not generally be regarded as the best place for decisiveness, but if he waited for the right time and place, he might wait for ever.

"Elizabeth, you've guessed how it is with me, haven't you? I'm pretty badly in love with you."

Elizabeth closed her eyes for a moment and lowered her cup to her lap. Then she stared fixedly at the coffee-pot. But she said nothing at all. The silence was depressing. Howard couldn't stand it.

"Don't say anything if you don't want to," he went on. "But if you think I'm just a dead weight of boredom and I ought to pack up . . ."

"No," she said. "It's not that."

There was feeling in her voice.

"Thank God for that, anyway."

Again there was silence. Howard congratulated himself that at least this was better than a vocal rebuff. Then, while his eyes traced the lines of the pattern on the carpet, Elizabeth's voice, quiet and controlled, reached him as from a distance.

"I know so little about you."

Howard's mouth curled upwards.

"That's true, I suppose, since you say it," he laughed. "But it's rather dismal news, considering that I've been advertising myself to you at full blast for the last few months."

"Perhaps that's the trouble."

"I see. Too much high-pressure sales talk?"

"Too much that has been forced and unnatural. It covers you up."

This gave him a jolt.

"You mean that I seem to be hiding something?"

"I didn't say that."

"I'm glad you didn't," Howard said, perhaps with a little too much relief and conviction, for thus he put an end to Elizabeth's analysis of himself, which he was just beginning to enjoy. Meantime he was left with the impression that she still regarded him as something of an outsider. And of course there was some justification for that. After all, he could see her against a certain background—the neat villas and trim curving avenues of Nunswood, All Saints' parish church, and that parson fellow, Cottesmore, with his black skirt and his pom-pom. But he had presented himself to her in detachment from any picturable background—an isolated specimen of mere maleness, torn from its context in the human scene.

"I know what you're trying to say," he said gloomily. "I'm too far away from your church-going crowd."

"I was trying not to say that." She spoke simply and candidly.

"That's what it really amounts to. And the odd thing is that I've been trying so hard to meet you without all that. It's you I wanted to know; not your friends and relations."

Elizabeth shook her head, but Howard forged on, not allowing her to interrupt.

"I'm in love with you. I'm not in love with the rector, or All Saints' congregation, not even with the deaconess, or whatever you call her. You can't blame me for wanting to know you apart from all that."

Elizabeth closed her eyes in an intensity of disagreement that chilled him.

"No, no. You can't do that. A person doesn't exist on her own. You can't really know anyone out of their own circle."

Which of course, Howard reflected, was as good as to say that he was unknown to her, because he appeared before her periodically out of the stream of life, only to disappear back into the stream again. It also seemed to imply that anyone who married her would have to take on the parish church too, and the choir-girls, and the Tuesday Bright Hour. It would be like taking on a missionary society.

"Look, Elizabeth,"—he was determined to regain the initiative—"you're real to me in a way that no one else is real. By comparison your churchy friends are phantoms. You could say good-bye to them for ever, and you'd still be real to me."

"No——" she began.

"You would. You'd still be the same."

Howard bit his lip. His desire to force the issue and put the maximum weight on his personal claim had pushed him forward so that he had said more than he had intended to say. But he hoped that his warmth would count in his favour. He looked up to find her eyes fixed on his face with an expression of puzzled yet inflexible tenderness too maternal to be fully comforting. For a moment she did not withdraw her eyes: then she suddenly put down her cup on the table as though she had made a decision.

"Howard, you don't know what you are saying——"

"I do. It's straightforward enough. Surely you understand. I love you exactly as you are, with your church thrown in. But if you became a Muslim to-morrow, I should love you just the same. It wouldn't matter that much." He snapped his fingers.

"I should be a different person."

"Not to me."

There was a look of real distress in her eyes now, but Howard could scarcely regret his own fervour, for she was revealing, even in rejecting his words, how much she cared.

"Don't blame me," he added quietly, "for seeing everything I want in you. I can't help it. It's all there. Everything."

Her lips quivered in accentuation of her distress.

"Howard, can't you see, can't you see? You talk of being in love; and the very words you use make it impossible for me to respond—to listen."

The very same revealing words made Howard simultaneously shocked at his own stupidity and overjoyed at his success. He leaned forward and took Elizabeth's hand between his own. She did not withdraw it.

"Elizabeth, I think I understand. I'm not saying anything very dreadful. Only that I love you. Everything else follows from that. If anything is important to you, it will be important to me too. That's what I mean. It will matter to me because it matters to you."

Her eyes were lightly moistened; but she smiled.

"It won't do. I'm sure it isn't right. I can't think what the rector or Canon Kirkbride would say."

Howard squeezed her hand.

"They'd say—'Marry him first and convert him afterwards.'"

"I don't think so. It isn't as easy as that."

"It's easier than you think. Say you're in love with me, and I'll start learning the Thirty-nine Articles to-night."

It was a false step. Elizabeth withdrew her hand, and turned her eyes gravely away.

"I think we ought to go now," she said.

2

"Come in, Roland," Gregory said. "Julia will be ready in a few moments. Nice of you to help like this."

Nice? Roland Tay smiled wistfully. Was it really nice of him? Scarcely. In fact, strictly speaking, it was none of his doing. He had suggested an evening out to Julia, having moved much closer to her during his first months at St Margaret's. He had come to feel that perhaps there was now that meeting ground between them for lack of which he had once failed to make headway with her. After all, before Canon Kirkbride converted him and brought him into the Church, no doubt Julia had regarded him as a bit of an outsider. No doubt she had seen him as quite unqualified to play the suitor. But now the situation was vastly different. They could meet now on a new footing. And Julia appeared to have made the most of it, by sheer sleight of hand exploiting (was that the right word?) his invitation in a totally unexpected way.

"*I* can't come anywhere with *you* next Tuesday," she had said charmingly, "having another arrangement, but *you* could come with *me*—that is, if you feel like it." "But of course," Roland had said with genuine eagerness. And then came the explanation. Canon Kirkbride had induced a trusted band of his church members to plan and embark upon a systematic visitation of every house in the parish. Julia was enthusiastic about the idea. Already she had put in several evenings. Why shouldn't Roland come and help her with a further assignment next Tuesday? Why not indeed? And so here he was, a fish out of water, a suitor, D.V., on evangelism bent.

"Here she is."

Gregory had not time to lead his friend into the drawing-room, for Julia appeared on the stairs.

"Good hunting," Gregory added, rapidly leaving the hunters to it.

Roland turned from brother to sister, marvelling, as he always did, at the lack of physical resemblance between them; he so big and shambling; she smallish, agile, trim. And, most unusually, she was to-night wearing a prim little hat which gave a touch of rather unwelcome sobriety and formality to the immediate prospect. Roland sought to cast off the weight of this threatened formality.

"I'm sorry to have come empty-handed. I searched the house for a banner, but I couldn't find one anywhere."

"I'm sorry too," Julia replied in kind. "I like of all things to be preceded by a banner. We have one upstairs: but unfortunately it would associate you with the Girl Guide Movement."

They laughed together: and Roland was heartened.

"There's only one thing worrying me now," he said, the left eyebrow raised half-whimsically, half-plaintively. "Shall I have to sing any hymns?"

Julia's hand was on the door-knob.

"We're going to make a series of social calls. We're not going to hold street-corner services. Come along."

Roland began to feel relieved. Perhaps it wouldn't be too bad after all. "Social Calls" sounded quite above-board. But nevertheless he was sure that religion must enter into it somewhere. It was best to be prepared for it.

"Am I to understand that we're just going to knock on doors, like Jehovah's Witnesses?"

"As far as possible, we try to knock like members of the established Church."

Out in the main road, they walked for some time in silence. Julia, not wholly inexperienced in Roland's character, wondered about his new interest in her. Was he falling in love with her? She thought not. Things didn't happen very decisively with Roland, generally speaking. He was a great one for lingering uncertainly on the brink. She suspected that he was tentatively exploring the possibility of falling in love. And, without any unfriendliness, she intended to keep well away from the edge. A girl looks for some conclusiveness in a man. If he lacks it, she is likely to treat him as a boy.

Roland, on his part, was asking much the same question about himself as Julia was asking. Was he in love? There was good reason to be, he thought, glimpsing by a side-glance the clear line of her profile, carved out of white stone against the drabness of the October night.

"Right turn," she said. "This is my terrain. Denvers Street. We take up at number 44. The even numbers are on this side. It's not easy to see them. We shall have to count the gates."

Roland turned dismally. The dim gas-lit side street

was quiet, and shadowed with great patches of blackness after the electric brightness of Park Road. They were alone and unseen. Her face was a steady white flame in the shadows: and they had to count the gates! Within five minutes, no doubt, they would be knocking at the first door and quoting Deuteronomy to some bored householder.

"Fourteen," he said aloud.

"Yes. A poor old man lives there on his own. Quite a hermit. It's rather sad. He's a bit of a misanthropist."

Embittered by neglect no doubt, Roland said to himself. Aloud he added, "I feel as though I'm on my way to the dentist's."

"It is rather off-putting—the first time. But you get used to it."

"Whatever does one say? I shall have to leave the talking to you."

"You can at first," Julia said.

Roland grinned.

"A bargain. I stick my foot in the door to prevent the victim from shutting it in our faces, while you open the Bible and fire the texts."

Julia laughed, a rather polite laugh, and touched Roland's arm in remonstrance. Roland was conscious of being touched for the first time: but the erotic quality of the gesture was nil.

"Be serious now. This is number 44."

They were great Victorian terrace houses, once the homes of prosperous middle-class families, now running that unsteady course between respectability and decay which, as Julia had already noticed, made it possible to expect anything of their inmates. A few still

18

housed people of some means who preferred large and shapely rooms to modern fitments in cramped quarters. Some had been converted into flats. Two at least had become boarding houses. And as the Upper Corton Milk Bottling Company had recently established its office premises in number 37, it began to look as though the tone of the street might soon descend further.

Julia and Roland had to climb six steps to the door of number 44, and unfortunately their reception was such that they descended the same steps a few moments later. Not that they were ignored. A thin-faced lady, somewhat harsh and manly of voice, opened the door six inches, and surveyed them as though they were claiming entrance to the harem of a tyrannical potentate.

Julia betrayed no embarrassment.

"We are visiting the parish, as members of St Margaret's church," she began. "We don't want to intrude if it's inconvenient."

Here she was interrupted by a single decisive word, uttered with a cryptic forcefulness.

"Chapel."

"Oh, of course," said Julia; "if you are already churchgoers——"

"Chapel," the voice replied again.

"I'm so glad to know," began Julia, betraying a touch of uncertainty at last.

"Good night," said the woman, and the door was closed.

They turned and descended the steps.

"Not a very auspicious beginning," Roland said.

Julia produced a notebook from her handbag, and proceeded to make jottings.

"Nonconformist. Name unknown."

"As for her family history," Roland said ironically, "she left us in the dark. The story broke off just as I was beginning to get interested. It's a pity. Perhaps you frightened her."

Julia sighed.

"It happens. Maybe I ought to have come alone. As we're together they might mistake us for crooks."

Roland cast his eyes down, as if to draw attention to his own slightness of build and gentleness of movement.

"Given a morbid imagination and an acute degree of shortsightedness, I suppose they might," he said.

Fortunately the two of them met with an altogether warmer reception at number 46. A middle-aged gentleman, probably in his late fifties, received them with suave cordiality.

"Come in, come in," he said, lightly stroking his head. "It's not a night for standing at the door."

They were conducted into a drawing-room, furnished distinctively with wicker chairs and Persian rugs. There were pink and white willow-pattern plates on a decorated japanned sideboard, and two Eastern fans were pinned above them on the wall. A Japanese screen, standing behind a carved Burmese writing-table, helped also to create an oriental effect. A couple of cheap Chinese aquatints, on either side of the fireplace, added something further. As the two visitors sat down, Roland felt it polite to show some appreciation of their host's obvious enthusiasm.

"You have been in the East?" he asked, sweeping the room with a glance.

"Unfortunately no. I wish I had."

The speech was slow, the articulation over-precise. The tone clear, light-coloured, unmodulated.

"Yet you have quite an Eastern atmosphere here, Mr—er?" Julia faltered cunningly.

"Pann is the name. Two N's."

"Miss Dean," Roland explained at this strategic juncture. "My name is Tay."

They all bowed their heads slightly as they sat, Mr Pann inclining his oval, moonlike face with all the gravity of an Eastern sage. The line of the eyebrows and the line of the hair alike swept down so as to emphasize both the egglike outline of the front-face and the dreamy wistfulness of the eyes.

"We are helping the Rector to keep the church in touch with the parish," Julia began, rather more vaguely this time. "St Margaret's is such a large parish; yet so thinly represented at our services. Perhaps you are a Churchman yourself, Mr Pann?"

As Julia spoke, Mr Pann tapped the finger-tips of his two hands together, and slowly, very slowly, shook his head, as if expressing on the stage an acute degree of ruminative detachment. He allowed a brief rhetorical pause before replying.

"Perhaps, Miss Dean, you know the saying of Sin Yo —'The gate of a garden openeth inwards, whether man cometh in or goeth out'?"

He stared hard at Julia, and Roland glanced, more sympathetically, too. It was plain that she neither knew the saying, nor understood its relevance. As she shook her head and tried to think of an appropriate reply, Mr Pann smiled indulgently and added a little more.

"Lee Fing has expressed the same thought more simply for us. 'You cannot catch the stars like butterflies, nor sweep the sky with a broomstick.'"

He nodded in some satisfaction, as though this were the last word on Julia's mission from St Margaret's; but clearly his attempt to simplify the wisdom of Sin Yo had not brought her much illumination. Sensing that, in some indefinable way, she had met her match, Roland began to feel secretly envious of Mr Pann, and even to wonder whether perhaps a short course in the sayings of Sin Yo might not qualify him better for pressing his claims further. But slowly she found her feet.

"I don't think I've ever tried to unhinge a gate, and when I sweep, I sweep the floor."

"I'm sure you do, Miss Dean. Except, if you'll pardon me, when you go to church and recite those presumptuous prayers and those insulting Christian creeds . . . No. I don't want to be asked whether they are true or not. It doesn't matter. Even if they're true, they're still presumptuous and insulting. Before Divinity we bow and keep silent. We don't waste our breath noisily telling Omnipotence what it is. Omnipotence does not feel the need of this information. Even if what we say is true, it is redundant and highly impolite. We have no right to shout out the obvious at the Eternal Spirit. Still less must we tell him lies. Either way he isn't interested. 'One man may raise a bucket from a well,' as Sin Yo says, 'but a hundred men cannot snare the sun with a rope.'"

"God is interested," Julia said simply. "He cares for each one of us."

22

Mr Pann raised his right hand gently to eye-level, as if he were very patiently calling to attention a group of lovable but tiresome children. When quietness reigned, he proceeded thus:

"Three poor scholars became impatient with their teachers, for they coveted the wisdom to understand all things. They put cloaks upon their backs and took staves in their hands, and they set out for a far country. Long they travelled, with much weariness and much wanting, seeking the renowned philosopher, Tzu Ho, whose words had power to wind up desires in the hearts of men and unwind riddles in the minds of women. And they came upon him in a barren country, seated upon a rock by the side of a stony road. So they fell down on their faces before him. 'Show us the light!' they begged. 'Only show us the light!'

"And Tzu Ho said to the first, 'Put your hand into the mouth of a fish.' And to the second he said, 'Bandage your eyes with a silken cloth.' While to the third he said, 'Scrape away the soil from the grave of your grandmother.'

"Now the three scholars murmured among themselves in dispute, till Tzu Ho rose from his seat and drew his mantle about him and said, 'I have shown you the dark places of the earth: and light is known in the breaking of darkness.'"

In the strange silence which followed this tale Roland could see that Julia was baffled. The feminine mind does not jump easily between the concrete and the abstract, and he realized that she would have difficulty in reconciling Mr Pann's previous utterances with the somewhat indelicate recommendation to desecrate a family shrine in the cemetery. A sudden chivalrous impulse urged Roland to take the responsibility for argument on to his own shoulders. He was now emboldened by the conviction that Mr Pann was much less wise than he thought himself.

"Perhaps you will think us very ignorant; but I hope you will explain this parable to us."

Mr Pann nodded very wisely as if to say, I thought so.

"The Ground of all being is unsearchable. We cannot look into the face of the One, nor speak to the One as to a fellow man. It is presumption to try. We shall find the One only in the oblivion of not doing."

"Not doing what?" Julia asked, rather naïvely, Roland thought.

"Just not doing," Mr Pann repeated, mouthing the words as though they formed a sacred charm. "Sin Yo has summed the matter up pithily. 'A man has five fingers on each hand, as the moon is wife to the sun; but he cannot shelter the dawn in his house nor call upon the twilight to sup at his table.'"

It occurred to Roland that Sin Yo's profundities presupposed a remarkable extravagance in human desires and aspirations. Julia thought so too. She had never been ambitious to entertain on the lavish scale alluded to.

"I'm sure Sin Yo was very wise," she said, "but I don't feel that his message touches me personally. I've never asked for the impossible."

"Ah!" said Mr Pann, drawing out the word on a long, laboriously instructive note. "But you invite your God to come down and sit in your church, while you ply him with the food of flattery. The wise man feels how his feet touch the earth, and he knows that he need never stoop lest his head scrape the sky."

"Is that Sin Yo?" Roland asked politely.

Mr Pann shook his head in modest deprecation.

"A little thing of my own. It has the true spirit of the sage, I grant; but he himself put the thought more tersely. 'The head of a man rests upon his shoulders, though the head of his horse rest upon the wind.'"

Julia began to think that evangelism was quite out of the question and she stole a glance at her wristwatch. Roland knew that she was not one to be easily defeated, but the task of bringing conversation with Mr Pann round to the point at which the claims of the established Church could be suitably pressed was clearly beyond her. Roland took the initiative on her behalf. He rose.

"Thank you, Mr Pann. It's been most interesting to listen to you."

"Very kind of you to ask us in," Julia said, rising too.

Mr Pann conducted the visitors to the door, cordial as ever.

"We have not done well to neglect the wisdom of the East," he said. "Now we are paying the price of that neglect in our present popular bewilderment."

From what he had heard, it seemed to Roland that the wisdom of the East would be more likely to increase popular bewilderment than to dispel it. But, rather weakly, he replied.

"Yes. We must think about that."

"Thank you so much," said Julia. "Good night."

"Good night, good night," said Mr Pann. "The rainbow is the handle of the earth. No man can climb it."

"Indeed not," Roland agreed. But Mr Pann smiled as though his visitors did not understand, before he finally closed the door.

Out in the street a wave of relief swept over Roland.

"Phew!" he said. "A horse has four legs, but you cannot pickle your great aunt with buttercups nor saw up the sky with a sledgehammer."

"Don't, please," Julia said. "I'm sure we ought not to. He was very kind. But whatever can I put in my notebook?" She rested her book on the gate-post; then began to scribble. "Non-Christian. Disciple of Sin Yo."

"We're not exactly winning souls by the thousand."

"Perhaps we came away too soon," Julia said, brooding. "We found out so little about him. We don't even know what he does."

"Nothing. He made that clear."

"You can't live on that."

"I gathered that you can't live fully in any other way," Roland said. "As a matter of fact, it was the one piece of moral advice which appealed to me personally."

At number 48 the visitors made an even slighter impact. A little boy answered the door, and Julia suggested that he might fetch his mother. When he returned, he said,

"Mother says she doesn't want anything."

"We are not selling anything," Julia explained, with a gentle smile, as the child stuck out his chin in an attitude of concentrated inquiry. "We have come from the church."

The boy scampered off without waiting for more. On

his second return he thrust out his hand and offered Julia a sixpence.

"Mother says thank you for calling."

"We are not collecting money. But since it's inconvenient," Julia went on, detecting the distant broken mutter of a TV programme, "we'll call at some other time."

Roland thought this would be the end; but he reckoned without Julia's zeal and resourcefulness.

"What's your name, sonny?"

"Tommy. I'm seven."

"You're a big boy."

"I should have said nine at least," Roland put in, hating to seem slow at improvisation.

"Do you go to Sunday school?" Julia asked.

"Tommy!" a male voice cried loudly from within, and Tommy disappeared. His next appearance was final.

"Dad says there's a draught. I've to close the door."

And father was immediately obeyed. That was that. Evangelization, even of the young, seemed to be out. The appropriate clerical work was done against another gate-post, while Roland looked in vain for some sign of fatigue in Julia.

"Not very friendly."

"They didn't understand why we've come," Julia said. "We never got into touch."

"There's something to be said for failing to get into touch at the door. It's more economical than failing to get into touch in the drawing-room."

"Three negatives," Julia said, unflaggingly. "We must achieve something before the evening is out. I'm

27

relying on number fifty. We've got to get inside this time."

They did get inside. An excitable little man, in his early thirties, introduced himself as Nathaniel Niblett, led them into the drawing-room, and drove out Mrs Niblett with an order for coffee and biscuits. Julia protested that this was unnecessary, but Mr Niblett replied that "the little woman" would have something ready in no time, and pressed the visitors into comfortable chairs before the fire.

"You must tell me all about it," he said, with an air of mystery, smiling encouragement as though they had come to relieve their consciences by some frank confession. At the same time he drew a chair up to the table, which stood between Julia and Roland, took a stiff-backed notebook from a drawer and, tapping his chin with a pencil, adopted the pose of one about to give a formal interview.

A questioning glance passed between Julia and Roland and, at its passing, a sense of more deeply established sympathy flickered into Roland's consciousness. It was delicious; but fleeting.

"I'm interested in everything that happens at St Margaret's," Mr Niblett was saying. "You must tell me all about this campaign of parish-visiting, and what you hope to get out of it. I want to get the whole thing clear." And he tapped his notebook with the pencil.

This seemed too good to be true. Roland could see that Julia was delighted to find someone who really wanted to hear what she had come about, and why.

"It was Canon Kirkbride's idea," she began, loyally

28

mentioning the canon as the mainspring of things. "He can't visit the whole parish; so a few of us are helping him. We want people here to realize that there *is* a parish church, and that it is *theirs*. That's our first aim."

Mr Niblett began to make jerky jottings in his notebook. This put an idea into Roland's head. It was corroborated when Mr Niblett looked dreamily up from his notebook and muttered, "Delphwick rector strikes blow for Church."

"Excuse me, Mr Niblett," Roland said. "Are you a journalist?"

Mr Niblett swivelled round and began to bounce lightly up and down on his seat.

"Nat Niblett," he said, "of the *Delphwick Evening Mercury*. I thought you knew. You must have seen the initials N.N. at the end of many a well-penned article, what! Don't you follow the *Portrait Gallery of Local Personalities*? And what about the *Nibblings*, eh? What about the *Nibblings*?"

He rolled his eyes in gleeful triumph. Indeed all citizens of Delphwick had seen the daily gossip column in the local paper. It represented a typical provincial attempt to emulate the alternately slick and verbose commentaries of the named columnists on the national dailies. This routine-mixed grill of allegedly urbane chatter was headed *Nibblings by Gnat*, and *Gnat* scrawled a spidery signature at the end of the day's assignment.

"Gnat," he said, as though the joke had just occurred to him for the first time. "Gnat. You see, Nat Niblett. It was Muriel's idea; honestly it was. You wouldn't think it, to look at the little woman, would you?"

As Muriel was busy brewing coffee in the kitchen and the two visitors had scarcely set eyes upon her, they could not do anything about this uncomplimentary remark. Besides, Roland was too preoccupied in looking at Julia, who was visibly taken aback. She had warmed to the first responsive parishioner of the evening, only to discover that his interest was merely a professional one.

"Go on," Mr Niblett said to Julia. "Rector wakes up sleepy parish. Laymen take Church to people. Novel answer to challenge of apathy."

The sparkle had gone from Julia's eyes; but she forced herself into action again. Even journalists have souls, she told herself.

"Parishioners are just not *aware* of their Church, Mr Niblett. If we who belong to it can get into touch with the people we live among, I think we can at least make them conscious of the Church existing in their midst. That would be something."

Mr Niblett swivelled round to his notebook again and he jotted with a new vitality.

"Gulf between Church and People," he muttered. "Bridging the Gap. Call to Modern Man." He turned his head confidentially to Julia. "Have you anything to say about Football Pools?"

"Nothing at all."

"You don't disapprove of them?"

"I've never thought much about it," Julia said reflectively.

"Church turns blind eye on Pools," said Nat musingly. "No, that's too strong. But it would bring in the letters. Sorry. That's the trouble with us journalists. We can't take our minds off our work. Do go on."

"Mr Niblett," Roland said, determined to be helpful. "You won't mind my saying so, I'm sure. Miss Dean has really come to see you as a fellow-parishioner, not in your professional capacity."

"Oh, quite, quite . . . er, Dean. Yes. Thanks for the name."

Roland frowned. His first contribution here and he had put his foot in it. Julia's name would be scattered among the Nibblings.

"We want to ask you personally, Mr Niblett, whether you have any religious interests yourself." Julia's face was so frank and her eyes so warm that Roland thought that any man of taste would have been ready in response to attach himself on the spot to any religion under the sun. Mr Niblett hesitated thoughtfully. Julia pressed home her appeal.

"We do want you to feel that we've come to ask a real personal question. Not that we expect a straightforward answer—or even an answer at all. It wouldn't be fair to expect that. No. We want to leave the question with you. Have I any religion? Ought I to have? That's all we want to say, isn't it, Mr Tay?"

Roland nodded weakly, inwardly aware that his thoughts in no way measured up to Julia's. He could admire her intense earnestness and marvel at her zeal. But he could not honestly pretend that he cared much for Nat or Gnat, with a religion or without one. Perhaps it would come later, that capacity to feel concern for others, a concern extending even to casual acquaintances. Certainly he could pretend to no such charity

31

yet. Meantime he felt there was something churlish about Nat's response to Julia's appeal, for he had returned, more pensively, to his notebook.

"Personal challenge straight from the shoulder," he said. "Man to man approach. Question of the hour. Does twentieth-century man need God? . . . If I may ask a question, Miss Dean, do you think there are too many divorces?"

"I'm sure there are. Every divorce is one too many."

"Church hits out at divorce," he began.

"Wait a minute," Roland said, foreseeing possible trouble. "You mustn't identify Miss Dean with the Church, you know."

"Quite so," said Nat. "A personal opinion. The woman's point of view."

Julia tried to get back to the subject of her mission.

"Divorce hasn't got much connexion with what I was trying to say; the question of your personal belief, I mean."

"Divorce issue irrelevant to Church's challenge . . ."

"Oh no," Julia protested.

"But I understood . . ."

At this point of confusion, the coffee and biscuits were brought in by Mrs Niblett, a woman who wore a down-trodden look which Roland for ever afterwards associated with journalists' wives. Both Julia and he tried to draw her into conversation; but it was difficult. For one thing, her husband was never silent for long. For another thing, Mrs Niblett betrayed a fixed habit of answering in monosyllables. Roland wondered whether she had developed this technique through the years as the only adequate defence against having her statements distorted into cryptic headlines or mistranslated into journalese.

Nat leaned sideways on the back of his chair, his left hand reaching backwards to his coffee-cup on the table behind him. Julia tried in vain to engage Mrs Niblett in conversation. Roland could readily guess what she was thinking. She might have done a much more fruitful evening's work had she managed to catch the housewife on her own.

"I wish you'd say something about the hydrogen bomb," said Nat, suddenly and naturally, as though armaments had formed the chief topic of conversation in the interview hitherto.

"What can I say?" Julia asked.

"Oh anything," Nat murmured. "Women and the H bomb. A message to mothers everywhere. Homemakers take stand against home-breakers. Eleventh-hour call to Nation's Womanhood."

It was becoming increasingly obvious that Mr Niblett required no external impetus from the world of fact to enable him to fulfil his professional duties with the needful éclat. Plainly he was capable of providing reports, leaders, and nibblings, all in total independence of the objective universe. It was something of a mystery to Roland why he should take the trouble to put questions and record answers, when his own inspiration was obviously quite adequate to his journalistic needs.

"Gambling is out at the moment," he went on, "unless you happen to feel strongly about Ernie? . . . No, I thought not. Vice isn't quite up your street. Teddy-boys are a specialist line. There's Smog, of course. November will soon be here. Do you feel strongly about open fires?"

"I'm appreciating this one," Julia said disarmingly.

"There's a *sort* of connexion with the Church," Nat murmured. "Must the Open Fire go? Symbol of English Home Life. What would Xmas be without the glowing hearth? Experts count cost in human lives."

Roland looked at Julia. Surely she had had enough. There was a mellow restfulness in her eyes as they met the blaze of the fire. He pulled himself forward in his chair as if preparing to rise.

"It's been very good to meet you, Mr Niblett, any-how. In future I shall savour the *Nibblings* with a new delight, after having personally met Gnat himself."

Then Roland wondered. Had he put his foot wrong again? Julia made no move. Had he been too hasty?

"I was hoping," she said, "that before we left we might have persuaded Mr Niblett to bring Mrs Niblett along to Evensong next Sunday."

Nat raised a finger and shook it playfully.

"Guarantee me a good paragraph, and I'll come. Get the rector to promise one really printable outburst in the sermon, and I'll come up on my hands and knees."

The thought of the Nibbler doing public penance through the streets of Delphwick set Julia laughing.

"I don't know what you consider to be a printable outburst," she said.

"Anything topical that will bring in the letters. Anything that challenges sufficiently to make people talk, without being so irritating that it loses readers. That's the great point. Sometimes it's a delicate matter to draw

34

the line in the right place. But we're always ready to tone an indiscretion down."

"Or up?" Roland suggested.

Nat nodded wisely; then suddenly assumed a sadder tone.

"The clergy are not hitting out as they used to. It's a pity. It's bad for the press; and bad for the Church. The Church needs the publicity. Why, quite often these days the clergy let a red-hot issue go stone-cold without exploiting it at all. Take smoking and cancer of the lung. The thing was front-page stuff for weeks; and the clergy didn't say a word. No wonder your churches are empty."

"Perhaps it isn't a matter that calls for ecclesiastical guidance," Roland suggested, tentatively providing an opening for Julia. But Nat didn't give her the chance to intervene.

"It was first-rate stuff. 'Rector hits out at Doctors.' A headline like that will always get the readers. It was handed to the clergy on a plate."

He nodded his head in rueful disappointment with the local ministers of the gospel for so neglecting the opportunities given by Providence.

Julia stood up, obviously having decided at last that there could be little point in staying longer. Nat gave a short little laugh, which expressed a knowing degree of patronage.

"Now you came to teach me something, Miss Dean. And I've taught you something instead. For there's no doubt what the present failing of the Church is. The Church is weak on publicity. You think that over, and ask the rector to think it over too."

He extended a magnanimous hand, as if bestowing upon the Church, as a friendly gesture, a free dose of expert professional advice. Within a few moments the two visitors were out again in the night.

At number 52 things seemed to take a turn for the better, when Mrs Badger, an aging lady, received the visitors with a warm smile and took them into her cosy kitchen. As Roland studied her gentle movements and kindly eyes, he concluded that here was the evening's greatest opportunity for Julia. And Julia thought so too.

"I'm so glad to meet someone from the Church," Mrs Badger said, poking the fire. "We live in such a wicked world. What dreadful things we see in the newspapers. It's sinful to have to read it all."

Roland wondered whether Julia would point out to Mrs Badger that she lay under no legal or moral obligation to read the daily paper from cover to cover. After all, it was with that kind of ruthless logic that Canon Kirkbride had first stirred him from his own scepticism and indifference. But of course Julia only smiled sympathetically, and Roland was not surprised. She seemed able to respond to everyone with the maximum of studied tenderness.

"These dreadful divorces," Mrs Badger went on. "And the terrible attacks on women. What things they do! And it's said the papers don't tell us half what there is to tell. A woman isn't safe out of her own home at night. I'm glad you are able to bring your husband round with you."

Roland rather enjoyed the brief moment of confusion which followed this misjudgment. A little too hastily

36

Julia said, "Oh, we're not married", and a look of curiously interested disapproval flitted across Mrs Badger's face.

"This is Miss Dean," Roland said. "My name is Tay."

"Perhaps you sometimes come to the parish church, Mrs Badger?" Julia inquired.

"Every year for the Harvest Festival. I do so love Harvest Festivals. I go to as many as I can. The parish church, the Methodists, the Baptists, and the Catholic Apostolics, and several more. It's a pity that some of them always clash. That ought to be avoided. Perhaps you will mention to the rector that it's not a good thing. This year he hit the same day as the Gospel Hall and the Congregationals. It spoils it for all of you."

"Perhaps you come at Easter too?" Julia asked, not eager to follow up this issue, and anxious to focus attention on some more significant occasion in the Church's year.

"I always go somewhere at Easter. Very often the Gospel Hall. They sing so cheerfully there. Of course this clashing of dates is much worse at Easter than at Harvest. I've often thought what a pity it is. All those churches, and all choosing the very same Sunday for Easter! Now if it could be spread over a few weeks, more like the Harvest Festival, it would give us a chance to go to one or two services and compare them. Everyone would benefit, I'm sure. I wonder if you could mention that to the rector too. The Easter hymns are lovely as well."

Roland could see that Julia was not much taken by this novel suggestion for staggering the celebration of

Easter in the cause of promoting healthy interdenominational rivalry. He sensed a deep discrepancy, perhaps a tragic discrepancy, between the fervour of Julia's evangelistic mission and Mrs Badger's frank desire to spend the entire year alternately ploughing the fields and scattering the Allelulias.

Julia looked at her hostess earnestly.

"I wish you felt that at Easter you liked to be in your own parish Church."

"Oh no." Mrs Badger was mildly horrified. "I shouldn't want to feel like that about it. It wouldn't be right to make distinctions. I must treat you all alike. It's the same with my grandchildren. If I give sixpence to one, I give sixpence to them all. That's what I said to Mr Coddring from the Baptists. Fair's fair."

This sublime superiority to interdenominational strife took the wind out of Julia's sails. She looked puzzled.

"You were baptized at St Margaret's?"

"Oh yes. All the family were christened at the church."

"But you don't count yourself a member of the Church now?"

"Oh yes. I'm a member of them all."

"I see." Julia was deflated.

"They're all going the same way," Mrs Badger added. "There's no point in quarrelling. I like a good sing. And I like a good pray, if it isn't too long-winded."

"Now," said Julia, making an especially sweet and confidential approach. "Tell me honestly which church you prefer."

"Well, there's something to be said for them all.

38

They sing very well at the Gospel Hall, and the praying is very natural and sincere at the Methodists. And I like the windows in the church. They make it seem more holy. But, you know, I think I like the wireless best of all of them. It has more variety. And I can sit in comfort from beginning to end."

"I see," Julia said quietly.

Perhaps she was prepared in advance with ammunition against the dissenting sects. Roland did not know. But plainly she had not anticipated having to counter the claims of this new denomination, the B.B.C.

"The various churches all broadcast their services from time to time," Roland said helpfully.

"Yes," Mrs Badger nodded. "That's why I like the wireless best."

Julia leaped in again.

"And which *service* do you like best?"

Mrs Badger reflected a moment.

"The Home Service."

The little trio seemed to be moving in a circle of misunderstanding. Julia made a decision.

"I shall ask the rector to call. I'm sure he'd like to have a talk with you."

Mrs Badger nodded.

"I've always kept up my church-going. Even if it has been only the Chapel in the Valley on the Light Programme. The Reverend Macpherson has a lovely voice. And he doesn't preach too long." She rose from her seat. "I must show you my scrapbook. I read a bit from it every night. The Bible is so hard to follow, and the print is so small. So I've made my own collection of holy words."

Thus it was that Roland came to have the opportunity of studying Mrs Badger's private anthology of cuttings from the literature of the age.

When you feel that life is all hurry and rush, and there isn't time to think; when your back is bent to the sweeping brush or over the kitchen sink; when the day seems long and the news is bad, and you feel quite sure you've really had as much as you can bear —then go to the doorway and look at the sun, and listen awhile to the birds; watch how the morning breezes run and hear their whispered words. Then bless the things that live and move and fill this weary world with love—just bless them with a prayer!

There was much more in the same strain. And Roland turned the pages with appropriate reverence as Julia chatted with Mrs Badger.

It isn't looks, however sweet, that makes for real success; it isn't even your Balance Sheet, and it isn't the way you dress. It's something deep, deep down within the shelter of your breast—the place where all your hopes begin and all your cares find rest. Sweet is the beauty of the face where loving kindness lies; and sweet in beauty, sweet in grace is the light in loving eyes: but sweeter still, beyond what art and outward things express—the beauty of the quiet heart, its inward blessedness!

It was plain to Roland that Mrs Badger drew her spiritual sustenance from material of questionable quality. He sat back, and looked over the top of the scrapbook at Julia and herself as they talked quietly together. There was a good deal of head-nodding on Mrs Badger's part, but he guessed that the agreements expressed represented no real understanding of Julia's appeal. How could they, after what had already been said? The Nibbler was wrong, utterly wrong. How could high-pressure sales-talk touch such as Mrs Badger? What effect would it have on her if the clergy for miles around hit out, nay lashed out, every week in the direction of front-page topics? She was untouchable. Completely happy, it would seem, with her daily readings and her serialized Harvest Festivals. Certainly not an unbeliever, nor a sceptic; yet equally certainly impervious to the pressure of Julia's appeal—miles away from conceiving of the Church as Julia and Canon Kirkbride conceived it, a body living in disciplined worship and sacrament, obedient to the claims of another world. It seemed almost irreverent to seek to disturb Mrs Badger from the comforts of her sentimental religiosity. Roland felt that it almost amounted to an irreverent interference with the very nature of things—an interference that offended one's sense of propriety. He had had this same feeling before when he had seen desperately extravagant and intensive efforts being made to teach extremely backward pupils to read and write.

There was no lack of fervour or of spiritual zeal on Julia's part; there was no lack of goodwill on Mrs Badger's part. Yet the two of them did not operate on the same wave-length. Communication was not effected. The patient yet strained bewilderment in Mrs Badger's eyes could never fully answer the generous assurance in Julia's.

Roland closed his eyes dreamily. The chapel woman, Mr Pann, harrassed little Tommy, Nat Niblett, and now Mrs Badger. Was it all, then, a waste of time? He was inclined to think so. An unselfish, almost heroic, waste of time on Julia's part; but nevertheless a waste.

3

"CANON KIRKBRIDE? Oh, good! How do you do. Jolly good! I hoped you'd be in. My name is Prentice. Howard Prentice, that is. You know, Prentice, March, and Prentice. That's the old man, of course. But I'm in on the racket too. Beastly cold, isn't it?"

Canon Kirkbride shook the proffered hand, and made a quick preliminary survey. Tall, thirty-fivish, aging about the temples, not yet about the eyes; volubility inordinately high—half showmanship, half nerves.

"Come in, Mr Prentice."

"Awfully good of you. Perfectly wretched time to burst in on a fellow. Hate evening jobs myself. I expect you get quite a lot of that kind of thing."

The canon silently estimated that it would take a quarter of an hour to reduce Mr Prentice to that condition of repose in which communication could be effected between them.

"Very novel for me, all this. I mean, you and me. Not that I haven't met people. As a matter of fact I've mixed an awful lot—and with all the usual brands. But contacts with the cloth just haven't come my way. Coincidence, I suppose. Thanks a lot."

Canon Kirkbride gave him, in turn, an armchair, a

43

cigarette, a light, an ash-tray, moving all the time with a quiet sacerdotal deliberateness calculated to shed tranquillity.

"Little matter of a wedding." Hand and cigarette waved in the air, trailing the smoke. "Well, you know how it is. It's been coming up for some time, as these things will. Frightfully nice girl."

Mr Prentice tossed his head. Indeed his conversation was punctuated by minute tossings of the head, which seemed somehow to imply that what was being said need not, if the audience were so minded, be taken too seriously.

"This wedding," said the canon slowly, feeling his way. "Am I to understand . . .?"

"Nothing out of the ordinary there. Just the regulation treatment. But there's no need to trouble you about that just yet—though I suppose you'll have to be there when the time comes, eh?" He laughed nervously.

The psycho-analyst, said Canon Kirkbride to himself, might conclude that Mr Prentice would prefer me absent.

"Mr Prentice, you are planning to marry . . ."

"That's the general idea."

"And the happy lady?" the canon queried tentatively, secretly doubtful whether her lot was in fact very enviable.

"Miss Lyte," said Mr Prentice decisively. "Miss Elizabeth Lyte, daughter of Mr Anthony Lyte, the estate agent. I think you know her."

"I do indeed." The canon's features stilled. He was suddenly very thoughtful.

44

"She was to have come along with me this evening to introduce me. But it's right out. A touch of flu, I'm afraid."

"I'm sorry to hear it."

"Nothing serious. Rotten luck, of course: but it might have come at a worse time."

The canon moved over to the table which served as his desk, and took out a notebook from a nest of small drawers beside it.

"Am I to understand that there is some prospect of my being asked to marry you . . . ?"

"Steady on, Padre, not so fast." There was a marked change of tone. "We're not there yet, I'm afraid. That's what I've come to see you about. It seems there's a snag."

"Oh?" The canon was not all that distressed to hear so.

"I'm going to be quite frank, Padre."

"Please do."

"Very well, then. This is all on Elizabeth's account. She's looking to a church wedding. I know she is. She sort of believes in it—the way people do. You know what I mean, Padre."

"Indeed I do. You forget that I know Elizabeth well."

"Quite so. She's been brought up like that. Well and good. But for me it's different. It's all one to me whether I'm married by you or the registrar or the brigadier in the Sally Army."

"I see."

The canon thought perhaps he'd better wait for more. And his patience was rewarded.

"Of course I wouldn't dream of disappointing Elizabeth over this. And that's where you come in. I understand that if I'm to marry in church I need to be christened—sounds a bit babyish, I must say."

"Baptized," said the canon.

"That's right. Well, anything to please Elizabeth. I gather it's simple enough. So what about it, Padre? Can you fit this little job in some time?"

The canon's hand went to his chin.

"You treat the matter rather lightly, Mr Prentice."

Prentice's hand swept the air.

"No offence, Padre. But I'm not going to deceive you into thinking I'm something I'm not. You're an educated man. You know how people look on religion these days. Well, count me in with the general drift. It's all so much guff to me. I suppose most of the folk you deal with to-day feel like that about it—even if they don't say so. A pity from your point of view, I know. You have your job to do, and it's not exactly a gold-mine."

"Hmmmmm." The canon's meditative sigh extended itself all the way from illumination, through reflection, to interrogation. "I suppose I ought to thank you, Mr Prentice, for not trying to deceive me."

"Quite all right, Padre." The hand was raised grandly, patronizingly.

"Of course I can't ignore what you've said."

"Don't take it to heart, Padre."

"What you've actually come for boils down, I think, to a request for baptism."

"That's right. Any time you like. Just put me through the drill."

46

The canon shook his head.

"You're in a great hurry, Mr Prentice."

"I'm trying to save you trouble, Padre."

"Thank you," the canon said unenthusiastically; and indeed his furrowed brow and tightened lips suggested that Mr Prentice had not been eminently successful in pursuing his professed aim.

As for Howard himself, he was wondering why events were not moving more quickly towards clarification and negotiation. It occurred to him that perhaps the etiquette required him, at this point, delicately to refer to the financial side of the proposed transaction.

"Of course I realize that you'll expect a fee, Padre. Whatever you say. I'm not poor. Anything reasonable. You fellows have to live."

Although the last sentence was spoken without any great conviction, Canon Kirkbride hoped that some generosity of spirit lurked behind the blundering discourtesies, and he discounted them accordingly.

"First I must make clear that the Church has a discipline in these matters."

Howard Prentice shrugged his shoulders. The canon cleared his throat uncomfortably.

"Mr Prentice, you have expressed views about the Church's faith which would make it difficult for any conscientious priest to conduct the ceremony you are asking for."

"Oh come, come, Padre. You mustn't worry about me and my views. They're nowhere in all this. I've told you before that this is to be Elizabeth's show. She's the one we're fixing all this for. I'm only sorry she wasn't able to come to-night. You'll do anything

Elizabeth asks you to, Padre. You're sure to. Men can't help themselves."

Canon Kirkbride sighed deeply. His mind went back ten years, to the early days of his ministry at St Margaret's, when Elizabeth was a dark-haired little girl of nine or ten. Brown-eyed, round-faced, she used in those days to wear a black dress with a trim little red and white collar. She was the same age as Julia Dean. He had prepared the two of them for Confirmation together. And Elizabeth had grown, under his eyes, into an unmistakably marriageable young woman. It was not at all surprising that the son of a Delphwick businessman should be wanting her for his wife. But it was odd, to say the least, that the matter should be brought to his attention in this brusque and unsatisfactory fashion. Of course he hadn't seen much of the Lytes since they moved over to Nunswood four years ago. Nunswood was away at the other side of the city. But David Cottesmore, rector of Nunswood, had told him only last year that Mrs Lyte and Elizabeth made their Communion pretty regularly at All Saints. And they still turned up very occasionally at St Margaret's for Evensong. Of course it was natural that Elizabeth should think of St Margaret's if a wedding was in the air. No doubt she regarded it as her "home" church.

"I've known Elizabeth for a long time, Mr Prentice. My earliest picture of her would probably look strange to you. It goes back nearly ten years."

The canon spoke ruminatively, as though unlimited time remained at his disposal for dealing with Howard Prentice's request. It was necessary to approach with patience a tangled undergrowth of mental confusion which only great patience would ever sort out. And it was necessary to create some footing on which he and this restless young man could meet and communicate. He looked hard at his guest. Was it wishful thinking on his part, or was the young man beginning to relax, and forsake the strenuously garrulous rôle which he had adopted on entry? The canon swung round in his chair and leaned forward towards his visitor. They were now face to face.

"Mr Prentice, how about a drink, so that we can talk over all this at leisure? I can offer you a beer; a Guinness if you like."

"Awfully decent of you." Howard Prentice looked and sounded as though he were going to refuse, but then he suddenly changed his mind. "Well, why not? Thanks, Padre. Make it a Guinness."

And so, within a few minutes, priest and rebel faced each other across the hearth with half-filled glasses before them and a mellow glow within them.

"Mr Prentice, why don't you like God?"

The canon chose his tactics deliberately, dispatching the Kirkbride dialectical missile without any preparatory softening-up. The choice was made after a thoughtful survey of Howard Prentice's face, which interested the canon more deeply every moment. For the weakness in the face—the thing that corresponded with his emptily assertive volubility—was his mouth. It would have been an exaggeration to call the front teeth protrusive: they were merely well rounded, and the curve was sharp enough to hint at a supercilious, histrionic complacency. But the keen eyes and the high

ow belonged to another character, magnanimous,
estless, and ready to get to grips. It was at this charac-
er that the canon chose to launch his question. It was
received with a shock of surprise that trembled on the
edge of laughter, and then stood firm.

"That's a very hard question, Padre."

"It was meant to be."

"You don't mince things, do you?"

"I try not to."

"I see."

"Well?"

As the canon awaited a reply, Howard Prentice
stared at the floor. Then he spoke with a new steadiness.

"I don't dislike God. I dislike religion."

"Isn't that the same thing?"

"A very different thing," Prentice began.

"Wait a moment," the canon interrupted. "You
will admit this, I think—that it is in and through religion that man makes contact with God. That's what
religion is: the activity of man in relation to God."

"Perhaps it ought to be that; but it isn't." Howard
Prentice sighed. "I suppose that's why I dislike it."

Canon Kirkbride put his hand to his forehead, closing his eyes for a momentary silent prayer.

"Mr Prentice, when you admit that religion ought
to be man's relationship with God and then claim that
in fact religion fails to be that, I suppose you are
making a distinction between good religion and bad
religion?"

Prentice nodded.

"You can put it like that, Padre."

"Good, we're making progress. Now, if a man says he dislikes eggs, he means that he dislikes good eggs, doesn't he? There would be no point in his saying that he disliked bad eggs."

The visitor smiled his acquiescence.

"The same would apply," the canon went on, "if a man told us that he hated opera. We should have the right to assume that he was expressing a dislike of opera well-performed by competent singers and instrumentalists, singing and playing in tune. He would not claim to hate opera merely because he disliked bad singing and playing by incompetent performers with no musicianship."

Howard Prentice smiled and nodded silently.

"You see what I'm getting at?" the canon went on. "To express a dislike of anything is to express a dislike of that thing in its good and healthy form. So that to hate religion is to hate good religion. And good religion is that which brings man into contact with God. We've already agreed about that. I'm afraid there's only one logical conclusion to all this. To dislike religion is to dislike the man-God relationship. You yourself are a man. A man's dislike of the man-God relationship surely amounts to a dislike of God. The man who dislikes religion dislikes God."

Howard Prentice stared ceiling-wards and the whites of his big eyes shone in the firelight.

"I once knew a fellow who did this kind of thing on the stage for a living. Only it wasn't arguments, it was hamsters. He'd tell someone in the third row of the stalls that he had something crawling up his sleeve. 'Come up here, sir, and I'll extract it.' Everybody laughed when the poor fellow's jacket was publicly removed to reveal the livestock. But of course everybody knew the thing had been planned and planted before ever the curtain rose. Still, it was good fun."

"But I'm serious, you see," the canon said quietly.

"Then you oughtn't to be," Howard laughed. "Some things don't deserve to be treated too seriously. Suppose I say that I dislike popcorns, and then a brain-trickster takes me up and proves, with five minutes of verbal acrobatics, that I've really expressed a dislike of paper bags. Well, what then? I may admire the trick vastly. I may be tickled to death by it. But one thing is certain. I shan't run off in a fit of zeal and start devouring popcorns by the half-pound. Oh no. So where are we? I've admired your argument. I've taken it in. It was pretty good. But we're still where we are. There's still something that I generally call religion, and I still dislike it."

The canon scratched his head. It would be too strong to say that he was baffled; but he was certainly very pensive. For one thing, he had quickly decided that argument with Howard Prentice, if it were to continue for long, would be likely to call upon all his resources. There seemed to be an irrational streak in the man; and yet it had a powerful thrust and "logic" of its own. Strictly speaking, there had been no rational reply to his own tight and challenging argument. Rather Prentice had burlesqued it, mocked it, and thrown it, as if thus discredited, into the dust-bin. It was a potent, if unscrupulous, argumentative technique, which no doubt left its manipulator feeling smug and assured.

"So far as effective communication is concerned," the canon said brightly, "we're in a bog. Let's climb out

52

on to dry land. I suggest we refrain now from using the word *religion* and go easy with the word *dislike*. When you consider my own calling, as a priest of the Church, and the things it involves me in, like prayer and worship and so on, then what are the things you disapprove of?"

"Things?"

"Yes, things—not people, but practices, attitudes, ideas, habits, and so on."

"There's quite a lot to go at there."

Howard Prentice was beginning to warm to the priest, as one does warm to men who are hospitable, clear-headed, direct and yet not impatient. And he felt that, at least while drinking his stout, he could not treat his approaches without some degree of gravity and grace.

"I'll be fair. I've never tried very hard before to get my ideas about the Church into words. But I should say that you Church people have got a whole set of attitudes and notions that are so much poison to me. The people who attend your church regularly may be decent enough. I'm not saying anything against them. But their brains are furnished differently from mine. Things they take for granted I have no use for at all."

"For example . . ." the canon pressed.

"Well, they think you clergy have special power and status. They think you can forgive them their sins and give them some sort of spiritual power. They think you have the right to tell them how they should behave— and to lay down the law about things like divorce. Well, that won't wash in a free society like ours. We're not going to be told where we get off by politicians

53

and bureaucrats, or by priests either. The whole set-up —priests and bishops and archbishops—is based on a reactionary view of society. No man has the right to interfere in another's private life. As for forgiving sins, it's nonsense. We can't accept these fancy, half-magical differences between one man and another. Joe Snooks isn't going to be a better man than I am simply because he has been hit on the head with a Bible by the bishop, and given permission to put on a night-shirt and stand in a pulpit. Sorry, Padre, but I feel quite strongly about this. I mean, if we don't take our freedom and our equality seriously now, what's the hope for the future?"

The canon's finger rested lightly against his lips. What indeed *was* the hope for the future? He wondered that too. But not because he foresaw the demise of freedom. Rather he glimpsed momentarily. in the dim future, the ultimate death of logic. Swallowing his distress, however, he smiled disarmingly.

"One minor point, in parentheses, before we begin. No provision is made, in the Ordination service, for the bishop to use the Bible in the way you mention. You're confusing the ceremony with something less sacramental, I think. Matriculation, perhaps, or graduation."

Howard Prentice laughed good-humouredly.

"Sorry, Padre, I was off the mark there."

"Now that we have cleared up that little confusion, perhaps we can turn to the main issue." The canon leaned forward confidentially, determined, before more was said, to expose his visitor's case to the light. "Let us make sure that I have understood your com-

54

plaint. You find something in the Church which is offensive to you as a man of liberal principles. In specifying what that something is, you mentioned especially the priest's authority to teach the word and to absolve the penitent. Is that so?"

"Quite right, Padre. That's what I said, and I'm sticking to it. No man can forgive sins."

"Well, let's take this troublesome business of our freedom and our equality." The canon spoke musingly with the air of one who has a problem to tussle with: as indeed he had, though it was not quite the problem Mr Prentice imagined it to be. "Is there something illiberal about the priesthood? That's the issue, isn't it?"

Howard Prentice nodded and, as the priest lingered on the question, concluded too readily that he had got the canon on toast.

"Mr Prentice, do you think there is anything illiberal about a judge sending a criminal to gaol?"

"Why, no."

"You think, in spite of human freedom and equality, that one man has the right to imprison another man for ten years or more of his life?"

"If justice demands it, yes."

"Justice?" the canon queried. "Is it justice in the abstract which justifies X in sending Y to prison? Are you sure? Suppose I know for a certainty that my neighbour has stolen my mother's jewels, have I the right to lock him up?"

"You haven't. No."

"But justice demands his punishment, surely?"

Howard Prentice frowned. He was beginning to get

tied up—not desperately so, but to a slight, irritating degree.

"I suppose," he said, halting now, "that it isn't just a question of having justice done, but of having it done by the proper people in the proper way."

"By the delegated officers in the established courts. Exactly. In other words, if I order Joseph Badman, the thief, to be locked up, that won't do. But if Mr Justice Black, sitting in the Frond Assize court, orders Mr Joseph Badman to be locked up, that is fine. But why this difference between Mr Justice Black and myself? Doesn't it offend your sense of human equality that he should be allowed to do what I can't do? Isn't it all rather illiberal?"

The canon's irony was unflavoured by any hint of aggressiveness: there was no sign of a sneer: rather his eyes glistened good-humouredly; and his voice wooed. Howard Prentice responded with a new frankness.

"Well, that's absurd, we know: but it's difficult to say why. I suppose the answer is that the nation has empowered Justice Black to punish offenders and it hasn't empowered you."

"True. That's a point."

The canon nodded: but nevertheless it was by no means the point he was wanting to get at. There was so much more. How get there in such a way as to carry his guest with him?

"Let me construct an imaginary situation, Mr Prentice. This judge of ours, Mr Justice Black—Timothy Black in private life—is not a very nice man. Let us suppose that, at home, he is a difficult, bad-tempered, selfish man, who makes his wife suffer a good deal by

56

his vanity and irritability. We will say, for purposes of argument, that he is a bad husband and a bad father, morally speaking. Of course, he never breaks the law; he is very careful indeed about that. But he is what ordinary decent folk would consider a rather nasty man in the home.

"Now Timothy Black takes his exalted place in the Assize Court one day and has before him poor Jane Jones, a widow, who has stolen money in order to give her six children a better chance in life. She has been, apart from this lapse, a woman of wholly admirable character, and it would seem doubtful whether she has ever been grossly selfish, vain, or bad-tempered in her life. Her theft is serious, because it involves a large sum and a gross breach of truth. Now, two questions. First, on the strength of this data I have given you, which do you think is probably the better human being, the superior being morally, Timothy Black or Jane Jones?"

"Jane Jones. I grant you that."

"Good. Now for the second question. Has Timothy Black the right to send her, his moral superior, to gaol?"

"He has the right. Yes."

"How comes it that a man can rightfully punish another man who is his superior in moral character?"

Howard Prentice was not in the least a dull or unperceptive man. And he was thus fully aware that, step by step, he was being driven towards a conclusion which would make mincemeat of his own earlier argument. Nevertheless, not being in the least a proud man, he did not try to hinder the canon's progress. On the contrary, he helped.

57

"Mr Black condemns the criminal in his capacity as a judge."

"Exactly."

The canon's face beamed with delight.

"As Timothy Black, Esq., of Hampstead, he has no more right to condemn Jane Jones than you or I have. But as Mr Justice Black he has every right. In the court he acts by virtue of his office. And the office gives him powers which are not affected by his personal character. That is why the existence of judges who condemn is consistent with the theory and practice of democracy; consistent with the doctrine of human equality. Because no man, simply *as* a man, ever condemns another. He condemns another only by virtue of his office. The distinction made between the person and the office is one of the most significant distinctions in civilized life. It is one of the keystones of civilization."

Howard Prentice began to think that Canon Kirkbride was about to make too extravagant a claim.

"So you clergy pretend to a kind of judicial authority. Is that what you're getting at?"

"Not quite," the canon laughed. "All I have done is to exemplify the distinction between the person and the office in a certain sphere. The priesthood is another sphere altogether. But there is the same distinction. The priest's authority is not a personal authority representative of a personal superiority. It is an authority of office. It is his by virtue of his priestly orders. As Michael Kirkbride, I dare not preach or teach, and cannot absolve or bless. As a priest of God's Church, I teach the Church's faith and administer the Church's sacraments. There is no point in telling me that

58

Michael Kirkbride is unfit to preach and teach, to mouth the words of absolution or to handle the blessed sacrament. I know that only too well. As Michael Kirkbride, I am totally unfit to exhort the sinner or to remit his sins; but as a priest of God's Church, ordained to that office, I speak the words of the Church and of God, to the forgiveness of sins and to the blessing of sinners, to the offering of our Lord's body and his blood.

"In a way it is odd that you should not have thought of this. For surely it is only in my capacity as priest that you would ask me to baptize you or to marry you. You have virtually admitted the authority of my office by coming to see me like this."

"Let's say Elizabeth has admitted it," Howard Prentice said, smiling.

"Whilst you . . . ." the canon pressed, for he was anxious that Prentice should commit himself.

Prentice tossed his head as if to return the question to the questioner. He was not going to be put on the carpet, stout or no stout. The canon's argument might be clever, might be valid—no doubt it was—but still this cleverness, this validity, somehow hung in the air, unattached to the sphere of practice and action. You're right, he was inclined to say; so what? That was the appropriate reply. So what? Be right, go on being right. Right, rational, logical, sound, just, fair. So what? But it would sound rude and crude to talk like that. The canon was magnanimous, and he was his guest.

"What does it signify?" he asked weakly, evasively. And the canon pounced.

"This. This is what it signifies. That the theory of the priesthood is wholly consistent with liberal and even with egalitarian notions. For the priest, as a person, claims nothing for himself in the way of virtue or authority. Only in holding the office of priest has he the right to speak and act with authority. This theory allows for the fact that the priest may or may not, as a person, be morally superior to those over whom his authority is exercised. As a person he may be a wicked sinner or a veritable saint. You don't ask which when he administers a sacrament. As a man, he confesses his share in man's common sinfulness. As a priest, he marries you, teaches you, and absolves you. How *dare* a man exhort others except in the name of a dignity not his own? How dare a man exercise power, except it be the power of an impersonal charge? How dare a man presume to rebuke or condemn, except in the name of institutional authority?"

There was silence for a time. Canon Kirkbride was silent because he had said what he had to say: Howard Prentice was silent because he couldn't think what to reply. He felt that the canon, merely by speaking at length, had somehow gained a point. He wanted to obliterate that impression, but he knew no argument for doing so. Therefore he used other means.

"You seem to feel quite strongly about all this, Padre."

This, said a little patronizingly, was intended to carry the vague hint that the speaker was one who could look down with detachment, as from a loftier station, upon the narrow sphere of the canon's emotive enthusiasms.

The canon, sensing a conscious evasion of rational discussion, remained silent, with half-shut eyes.

"Of course," Howard Prentice went on, "I'm not denying that this view of what a parson is exists, Padre, and I'm sure you hold it sincerely. Don't mistake me there. But still I find it a bit hard to swallow. You say the parson claims nothing for himself personally in the way of status and so on; but still he *appears* to claim a good deal. I mean, look at the things the clergy wear; the way they dress up; surely all that gives the impression that the clergy think themselves different. You can't strut about like a peacock and at the same time put in a special claim to be humble."

"Why not?"

"Oh come, come, Padre. It just doesn't make sense."

The canon twice removed and replaced his glasses with great rapidity. Prentice was indeed an awkward customer with little respect, apparently, for the laws of logic, when they happened not to subserve his case. He was an adept wriggler. And the canon might well have decided to let him wriggle out of his orbit, but he had a special duty to Elizabeth. Besides, something about the man stirred his compassion and called the rich resources of his patience into play. Partly it was Prentice's eyes. For all the flippancy proclaimed in the frequent tossings of the head and gesturing of the long hands, and for all the supercilious arrogance hinted at in the light laughs and in the play of the lips, there remained in his wide, earnest eyes the sad gravity of the soul at a loss which knows itself so.

"Is it to exalt himself that a policeman wears a uniform? Is that his vanity, his pride?"

"No. Not in that case."

"Why not?"

"Because the uniform shows what the policeman is and . . ." Prentice fumbled for words.

"And in what capacity he acts," the canon suggested.

"Yes."

"Good. That's it. The uniform helps to make clear to the thief that it is not Herbert Archibald Jameson who is arresting him, but an officer of the law. The person of Mr Jameson is not magnified by the uniform. Rather the uniform ensures that the person is swallowed up in the office."

Prentice nodded.

"In the same way," continued the canon, "the priestly vestments make it clear that it is not just Michael Kirkbride who is leading the worship of his congregation, but a priest of God's Church. The vestments do not magnify the individual person. On the contrary they indicate that the person is submerged in the office. No. Argue against vestments, if you want, on the grounds that plainness is preferable to finery. But don't argue that vestments trick out Michael Kirkbride, making him a show. They don't. They obliterate Michael Kirkbride, making him a priest."

Howard Prentice was not stupid. He knew when he had been proved to be in error. When the daylight came, he could see that he had held the wrong end of the stick. And, loth as he was to give ground before others, he recognized the point at which continued open resistance became the badge of stupidity. Nevertheless long ingrained habit prevented him from simply admitting himself wrong. He was one of those men who manage to receive gifts while wearing the air of a benefactor, and to concede arguments with the flourish of a victorious advocate.

"Well now, Padre, suppose I give you this point now,"—it was the voice of a trained bargainer—"suppose we say there's nothing arrogant about parsons and bishops dressing up and telling the rest of us where we get off, like a pack of school-children. Well now, what difference does it make?"

"I don't know what difference it makes," the canon said rather coolly, "but it happens to be the question we were arguing about."

Prentice frowned. So what? Where did it get him? Or where did it get anyone? Was there not something suspicious and discreditable in the very tidiness of these pat arguments? Was it not a kind of methodized lunacy? Theory of this; theory of that. What to do and how to do it. What not to do and where not to do it. Here all sit; there all stand; here the people kneel; there the people bow; here all sing; there all shut up. Tabs on everyone, rules for everything, from not marrying your grandmother's husband to fixing the date of Easter in nineteen eighty-four. Wilt thou, George, take thee, Patsy? To have and to hold. To love and to cherish. BUT NOT TO BE TAKEN AWAY.

"I get your point," Prentice said, pensively, as though there were still a bit of haggling to be got through before the transaction between them could be clinched. "But that's not the end of the matter. It isn't even a beginning. You can't turn a fellow like me into a church-goer with a neat little theory in defence of dressing-up."

63

"My immediate ambitions were more modest than you imply." The canon smiled quizzically. He had no wish to see the discussion clogged up with personal prickliness.

"Quite so, Padre," Prentice laughed. "We can agree to differ. Only I wanted you to understand that, on my part, there's much more to it than that. The whole system of church services goes against the grain with me. I've nothing against people praying. I'm sure there's such a thing as feeling God about you. No one who has been out alone in the hills or under the stars would deny that. It's something deep in a man that is touched then. That's the real thing. And I'd be the last man to make fun of it. But it's got precious little connection with what goes on in church. I mean it's spontaneous and free and natural. But institutional religion is different. Everything in church services is artificial and formal. All that mechanical repetition of stereotyped prayers, week after week, year after year; why, it's the death of anything sincere and vital. It's the blind opposite of true religious feeling: it's moribund and archaic. The genuine article is free and fresh as the wind."

For a few moment Canon Kirkbride's hand went to his forehead. How should he answer? What should he select from a bunch of fallacies, errors, and half-truths, which clustered as thick and close as grapes? What word among the dozen which Prentice had just misunderstood, misused, and misapplied, should he pick out for the honour of a public decontamination? The wise words of a former teacher came back to him. "My son, never answer two questions at once. Never correct two errors at a time. There is such a thing as intellectual patience, and a little of it is worth a mountain of brilliance." That was how Fr Folkes had put it over twenty-five years ago—Fr Folkes, slight, bent, myopic, peering round at an afternoon seminar in the summer-house; that strangely symbolic summer-house, deep in the college garden, half-way beween the chill, ascetic refectory and the lazy river bank.

"Mr Prentice, I disagree with so much that you say."

"I'm sure you do, Padre."

"So you won't make any mistake, will you?—you won't think I'm agreeing with the other things, if I neglect them all and just concentrate on one little point?"

Howard Prentice laughed, more naturally, less nervously, than the canon had yet heard him laugh.

"Padre, I assume in you a wholesale opposition to every word I say."

"Fine." The canon rubbed his hands. "Now perhaps we shall really get somewhere."

Prentice drained his glass of stout and the canon's finger danced in and out of the bowl of his pipe as though it were preparing the non-existent tobacco for a non-existent match.

"It's this idea of yours that there is some kind of opposition between things which are repetitive and formal, like church services, and things which are vital and sincere, like true religious belief."

"Absolutely. True religion should be a life-giving thing. Your church services are too mechanical and systematic. There's nothing life-giving about them."

"I wouldn't want to claim that we glow with fervent

devotion to our Lord," the canon said. "And of course we ought to. But I'm afraid we shouldn't be likely to improve our Christian witness if we cut down our Christian worship."

Canon Kirkbride's musing tone was so yielding that Howard Prentice began to think his argument was not going to be answered. Indeed for a moment the canon seemed to be taking evasive action.

"Mr Prentice, are you blessed with a good appetite?"

"Very."

"And a good digestion?"

"Cast-iron stomach." Howard laughed.

"You enjoy your food?"

"Every mouthful."

"Three solid meals a day?" The canon's smile was that of a fellow-conspirator.

"And some."

"Good. All the usual things, I suppose. Cereals, bacon, and toast for breakfast; a three-course lunch, and so on?"

"Standard English menus suit me fine," Howard admitted, secretly relieved to find the conversation drifting in a less earnest direction. "I'm rather heavy on the meat. Keeps my weight down."

The canon nodded.

"I just wondered whether you regarded this rather mechanical daily sequence of breakfast, lunch, and supper, as rather drab and undignified. It's something of a repetitive routine, isn't it?"

"I suppose it is." Howard sensed at last whither the canon was leading him.

"Yet you would admit that this daily stoking up is, after all, quite a *life-giving* activity?"

The two of them laughed at each other as the canon thus repeated Prentice's own word.

"I get you." Prentice was not anxious for the canon to rub his point in. But the canon was persistent.

"Rather like brushing one's teeth every morning. A tedious business really, but it keeps our teeth in good shape. Washing, shaving, dressing; cornflakes, tea, toast; there's an awful lot of mechanical repetition in life. But these drab routines do have their value."

"All right, Padre. You've made your point."

"I don't think I have yet. You see I do agree with you that there's something about routine and repetition that goes against the grain with us inwardly. That's very true. Take this business of nutrition, by which we keep ourselves alive. Eating and drinking can be pleasant enough. But it's a bit undignified to be so dependent on food and drink. And there are even more undignified things we have to do every day to keep fit. It's not all fun and poetry being a human being. You don't protest against these routines, these indignities?"

Howard Prentice shrugged his shoulders.

"We're made like that, Padre."

Slowly, deliberately, the canon repeated Howard's words.

"We're made like that."

Howard Prentice received this in silence, so that Canon Kirkbride began to think he must be getting bored; but in fact he was now recognizing fully that the canon knew what he was talking about and, on his own subject, the Church and its ways, had arguments at his finger-tips to defend and justify everything he thought and did. This being the case, to rake up the stock arguments against Church theory and practice was merely to bring a well-oiled dialectical machine into play which could chew up the fragments of current anti-clericalism without the slightest difficulty.

"You've got all the answers, Padre. Quite an entertainment to see you trotting them all out."

The canon stirred in his seat and a flicker of doubt, perhaps of self-questioning, moved over his face.

"I should be sorry to be regarded as a quiz-merchant, still sorrier to be regarded as a clown . . . And yet, I suppose, in the eyes of God, we are all something of the kind—puffed-up little actors and actresses, strutting and posturing on the stage of life. Which of us is not playing a part—and playing a false part at that—for a quarter, a half, three-quarters, or more of his waking-hours? It's a solemn thought. Yet that is what God has to look down upon. That is what meets his eyes when he gazes, as he must gaze, into every corner of human life. So much deception and self-deception. He sees it all and at once. And he sees it always. Simultaneously and eternally hears the lie on the lips and sees the truth in the brain behind them. That is the kind of God we are up against—or down on our knees before. Always watchful, present, informed, undeceivable. No pretence, no hypocrisy, no deceiving of others and no deceiving of the self can hide the truth from him. He knows what we think in our darkest broodings. He sees what we are in our most hidden ways."

And it was this, thrown out so randomly, so fortuitously, which lingered persistently in the mind of Howard Prentice long after this little interview was ended. Not the crisp arguments about the nature of religion and the distinction between the person and the office. Not the neat proof that there is nothing illiberal about hierarchical Holy Orders. Not the case for formal worship. None of these, so much as the canon's rambling reminder of how man stands daily exposed to judgment. A reminder by which the good priest's guided intuition answered the spiritual need of the moment.

It lingered with Howard because it was disquieting, unnerving. He would rather have thought of God in any other capacity than that of the eternally watchful spectator from whom nothing on earth is hid. He would sooner imagine a God apocalyptically enthroned in judgment after the demise of nature and the end of time, than entertain a momentary sense of the ever-present, divine, all-seeing Eye. Not that he often had cause to think of God in any capacity whatever. He hadn't. He was not a man who wanted to think of God. He was not a man who liked to be invited to think of God. For, lacking the comfortable assurance of the atheist, and temperamentally incapable of the easy evasions of the supposed agnostic, Howard Prentice found it necessary actively to fob off any suggestions of human connections with the outer and the other standing over against our little world. He had in fact developed a rapid little system of defensive reactions which came automatically into play when the smell of divinity was wafted even remotely his way. It took the form of a brisk patter, compounded of flippancy and sham cynicism. Canon Kirkbride had of course brought it fully into play, as we have seen. But its "fullness" was relative only. Since it was not rooted deeply in Prentice's character, it operated only intermittently. There was a tap on his brain labelled *Anti-Church Chitter-chatter: turn on only in case of emergency*. Emergencies were not frequent, but Canon Kirkbride had provoked one. And the tap had spouted and spurted into their evening colloquy, periodically directing a chill jet in the canon's face.

But, though the jet had played, the canon's words lingered, refusing to be washed away. No deceiving can hide from God what we are in our deepest broodings, in our most hidden ways. Everything stands crisp and stark in naked exposure before the All-seeing Eye. That kind of thing gives one the creeps, Howard said, supine in bed, addressing the ceiling. For even the ceiling was no defence against omnipotence. Old Fergy, mathematics beak down at Woolham, had once tried laboriously to make the upper threes understand that. How a being, inhabiting a four-dimensional environment, would presumably have the ability to see the inside and outside of a mere three-dimensional house at one and the same time. Howard couldn't remember how or why; though the case had seemed impressive at the time. But a clear image remained in the brain, left over from Fergy's brief excursion into metaphysics. An eight-roomed house with walls, floors, ceilings, roofs, all made of glass. Inhabited by men and women through whose transparent clothes and transparent flesh one could glimpse the organs and bones and muscles—slightly more opaque, of course. Frosted glass entrails within a clear glass case.

That was the funny side of it. And the other side of it was—just Mildred. Nothing very sensational. Nothing criminal. He hadn't robbed a bank. He hadn't poisoned a maiden aunt. But there *was* Mildred. An absurd thing to worry about, he would have said earlier —and so it was. Yet since he had got so serious with Elizabeth, it had seemed to matter more. And when they actually got engaged, it all began to assume the character of a dismal and irritating cloud overhead. And now, when Canon Kirkbride started to flavour the nuptial plans, at their very inception, with solemn talk about everybody acting a part and about God's all-seeing eye, then somehow the image of Mildred became oddly ubiquitous. He fancied, grotesquely, that perhaps she might become concretely ubiquitous too: hovering behind him at the taking of vows; awaiting him behind the door as he took his bride home. Why did he have to feel like that? Not in love with Mildred, not that now by any means; not particularly sympathetic towards her—she had killed all that herself pretty ruthlessly—but somehow carrying her about with him? Secretly burdened with an unwanted share of her for the rest of his days?

Meanwhile the canon had naturally been on the telephone to Mr Lyte. Yes, it was true that Howard Prentice was engaged to Elizabeth. No, it was not true that there was any question of an immediate marriage. Mr Lyte had himself reluctantly agreed to the engagement only on the understanding that actual marriage was not contemplated during the next twelve months. (Then what was the point of the engagement? the canon wondered. Wasn't an engagement an engagement to marry?) Mr Lyte did not want a row with his daughter; and he did not want to drive her to do anything silly; but most emphatically he did not like young Prentice. The fellow was too casual by half; and too conscious of being in the money. He and his wife still hoped that this affair might die a natural death.

Elizabeth was indeed in bed with flu. And he wasn't prepared to start arguing with her just now. It was typical of Prentice to come bursting in on the rector like that. No doubt Elizabeth had mentioned the necessity for baptism. She had always been a bit worried that Prentice was not a churchman.

No, it was not always easy to know how serious Prentice was being. That was one of the things they had against him. But, to be fair, one had to admit that much of his bluster was sheer nervousness. He had a better side.

Yes, Mr Lyte insisted, Prentice was always trying to stampede people. That was how he had brought off the engagement. If he got a chance, he would try to bring off a marriage in the same way. Baptism was just a necessary preliminary. He himself disliked Prentice's pushfulness. Why should the fellow be in such a fatuous hurry, anyway?

Why indeed? That was what the canon, too, badly wanted to know.

4

"YOU LOOK down in the mouth," Roger said.

"I feel it." Howard responded with some enthusiasm.

"Come into Fratti's for a drink."

A few moments later the two of them forsook the pavement of Towngate, Delphwick's busiest shopping street, and Roger steered Howard down a brightly-lit staircase. Apparently Fratti's existed at basement level. Roger stooped on commencing his descent and stooped again on arriving at drain-level. Not that it was in the least necessary to stoop. Although he was tall, the door-ways and passage-ways could easily accommodate his height and much more. But he had formed a habit of stooping momentarily on entering, leaving, or moving about unfamiliar, and even some familiar, premises. Howard had to admit that it was an impressive gesture. It suggested that Roger felt himself to be moving about in a world constructed on too small a scale for him, that he could all too easily forget the comparative small-ness of other human beings. Along with this habit of dodging imaginary ceilings and lintels went an habitual gesture, not at all uncommon, but peculiarly expressive in Roger's case. On sitting down, he invariably smoothed his right hand over his already smooth black

73

hair. At once casual and automatic, this gesture seemed to allow for the possibility that, even after all his precautions, some unnoticed hanging lamp-shade might have disarranged his hair.

"It's a cosy little place," Roger said; and when they had finished with corridors flanked with painted hardboard, Howard saw that it was. That is to say, it was dimly lit and there were chairs to sit on. Roger got the drinks and held Howard's out to him like a glass of medicine, putting on the air of the family doctor who has come to deal with a troublesome ailment that happens, for once, to be well within his competence.

"Now, what's the trouble?"

"Bad news."

"Really bad?"

Howard shrugged his shoulders.

"Conrad is going to divorce Mildred."

"Well, you're not legally obliged to marry her. Not even morally obliged. If you don't mind my saying so, old man, I don't think she wants you anyway."

"That's not the point," Howard said. "The divorce itself is neither here nor there. I've known for some time that it was in the offing. But naturally I assumed that Mildred would divorce Conrad. Well, it's going to be the other way round."

"Does it make any difference?"

Roger still spoke as though the whole matter were one that could be lightly shrugged aside.

"I shall be named as co-respondent."

"What of it? I shan't cut you in the street. All my best friends are co-respondents. In fact," he went on, putting his hand to Howard's shoulder and speaking

74

confidentially into his ear, "I make it a condition for membership of the inner circle."

Then Roger's jaw dropped suddenly. The penny had dropped too.

"Oh I see." He spoke thoughtfully now. "The Lytes don't go in for co-respondents in the family circle."

"Exactly."

Howard was emphatic. Roger frowned.

"And I suppose Elizabeth could be a bit fussy about that kind of thing herself?"

"*Could* be! If I know Elizabeth, she *will* be."

"Hmmm."

Roger indulged in a long, slow, pensive drink. Then he delivered himself of his advice.

"You must beat Conrad to it. Marry Elizabeth before the news is out."

"No good."

"Surely you can work quicker than the lawyers."

"Not this time. I tried to hustle things: but it can't be done. There are too many difficulties."

Howard was in no mood to try to explain them. For one thing, Roger would not be sympathetic. For another thing, he could not make clear to someone else something that was not clear to himself. This connection between religion and getting married was a bigger thing than he had thought it—bigger in Elizabeth's eyes than he would ever have dreamed, and therefore, no doubt, bigger in her parents' eyes too. Moreover, in spite of his attempted cavalier treatment of Canon Kirkbride, the canon had made him feel, uncomfortably, that there was more in Christianity than met the eye of the casual outsider. More, that is, for the people who believed it—even for people like the Lytes who did not ostensibly advertise their church-going to all and sundry.

How explain? It wasn't that he had suddenly begun to suspect that Christianity might be true. That kind of worry didn't occur to him for the simple reason that he had never seriously held the view that Christianity was false. Rather something that had looked scrappy and woolly and trivial had suddenly begun to look potent, coherent, and all of a piece. It was something that had depth; it was explorable, even by intelligent minds. That was the result of listening to Canon Kirkbride. Christianity was not, after all, something rather trivial plastered on the top of ordinary life—an icing of incongruous sentimentality—but something threading its way consistently through day-to-day thoughts, actions, and attitudes. So that, when you came up against Christians, you had to reckon with it. And when you planned to marry a Christian, you had to reckon with it in a big way.

It was all too serious for the honest man merely to ridicule it. It was also too unified and complex for the intelligent man to tamper with it lightly. An evening with Canon Kirkbride would not necessarily convert a fellow; but it certainly was enough to show that if you pried into religion you were in danger of getting into touch with something pretty big. It had roots. And it had a shape.

"Haven't you any allies in the camp?" Roger asked.

"Mrs Lyte has always been very decent. I think she likes me. But she's the kind who likes everybody."

"And the old man?"

"Not so sure," Howard said dubiously. "He's always been polite of course. But he doesn't know anything about Mildred. I think he's the kind who could come down heavily—especially if he thinks his daughter has been—well, er . . ."

"Well, what?" Roger pressed brutally.

"Insulted. That's the way he might look at it."

Roger laughed.

"If you want to marry his daughter, being a co-respondent ought to help, not hinder. After all, it's a kind of testimonial, isn't it?"

"Not in their world."

Roger tilted his chair backwards and lightly fingered his lapel as if he expected to find a carnation in his button-hole.

"If the old man has been remotely on your side, you ought to make a bee-line for him. Win him over on the moral question, and settle everything else with Elizabeth. Any decent old man will warm to the penitent rake. 'My only lapse so far, sir. It's taught me a lesson. Good of you to be generous about it.' Every decent old man likes to be generous."

To a certain extent this advice chimed in with what Howard had been thinking himself. But he knew that it was a good deal easier to make plans over a beer in Fratti's than to execute them in the sober atmosphere of Elizabeth's home.

"Why can't Mildred divorce Conrad?" Roger asked.

"She could. But she's rather enjoying not doing. So is he. I'm not popular with either just now."

"It's not gentlemanly," Roger said, brushing tobacco ash from his trousers. "He's a cad."

"I don't think it matters a damn to him—divorce, I mean. His women are not that type. They don't make conditions."

"Then it ought to be easy to fix something on him."

"It would be. But it's too late now. And I tell you Mildred is quite happy to have it like that. She might get her photo in the papers."

"Yours too?"

"That's the game."

Roger gulped down the rest of his beer and then went to replenish the empty glasses. Howard caught the eye of a solitary girl, elbows on table, face cupped in her hands, who was blowing cigarette smoke straight at him from the far side of the room. She was blonde, and going to be fat and middle-aged within the next few years. She looked as impatient as he was himself.

"Talk of the devil," Roger muttered, returning with more beer. "By the way, three bob. Your turn."

Howard paid him and Roger sat down again, not forgetting to smooth his hair.

"Can't you see. He's just come in. On the left there."

Howard saw soon enough. It was Conrad. Or rather Conrad's back. But he was bound to see them before they could get away.

Quite apart from the fact that Conrad was still officially Mildred's husband, Howard had several reasons for disliking him. For one thing, Conrad was eminently dislikeable. He always tried to take control of other people's conversations. He liked to hear himself talk and hated to hear other people talk with a passion. He was supercilious and unimaginative. He was of medium height, and more or less the same width all the way up, rather like a lamp-post. His bald head, extended horizontally by prominent ears, seemed to stretch almost the full width of his narrow shoulders. He ran a city hotel which made money effortlessly. His father had built the business up, and it would stand several generations of Spruices in good stead, however little work they might do, and however stupid they might turn out to be.

As soon as Conrad had turned from the counter with his drink, he caught sight of Roger and Howard, and he descended upon them in a characteristically proprietorial fashion.

"My dear Howard, this is a great pleasure."

Conrad always spoke in a slightly raised and stagey voice, as though he wanted some additional person to hear whom he knew to be in hiding behind the nearest door, with ears glued to the keyhole. He had too an irritating habit of rounding off his more significant sentences by pushing his tongue forward and lightly wiping his underlip. It was the gesture which some men use to give public notice that they have just enjoyed something good to eat or drink. Apparently Conrad used it to indicate that he relished his own statement, and to draw attention to its importance.

"It's something of an occasion."

He beamed; and his tone and bearing suggested, as they so often did, that what he said ought to arouse both astonishment and curiosity. There was an implicit challenge to further inquiry. Sensitive people detected the challenge and tended to resist it. Thus neither Roger nor Howard gave Conrad anything beyond a polite greeting and an invitation to join them at their table.

Conrad turned the full force of his unbounded assertiveness upon Howard.

"Would it be impolite to ask after my wife?"

"It wouldn't be impolite," Roger butted in, "but it would be rather out-of-date—as you know well enough."

"No, really!" Conrad said in that tone of feigned astonishment which readily admits that it is feigned. "She's proving too much for you, is she?"

He said it grandly, and Howard hated it. Conrad always seemed to treat him with a faintly patronizing air, as though he had done him a favour without really intending it. He tended to address Howard with that air of quiet but knowledgeable superiority which you display towards the fellow who bought your old car twelve months ago and is still not making a success of running it.

"Well, as I told you from the start, Mildred is a good girl; but she will not be neglected."

"I understand," Howard said coldly.

Conrad nodded wisely.

"I'm sure you must have learned a lot from her. But do tell me. Have you broken it off?"

"There was nothing much to break off," Howard said, lying pointlessly.

"Now that's the wrong attitude to take," Conrad said, correcting him magisterially. "You can't make love to Mildred without tying yourself in a knot which takes a hell of a lot of unravelling. Mind you, I'm not blaming you. She asks too much. She breaks the

80

camel's back. Some women are cut out to be mistresses; others to be wives. Mildred is neither. She's a career; a full-time job. A fellow can't stick the pace. Nothing could really stand up to Mildred except an organized trade union."

It occurred to Howard that there were other people in the world too against whose encroachments perhaps only an organized resistance could prevail. But he nodded wearily and said nothing.

"Well," Conrad said, "don't talk if you don't want to. Every man has the right to change his girl friend without advertising it. I'd be the last person to deny that."

Howard began now to feel as though, by remaining silent, he was letting the side down. As though, by not replying, he would acquiesce in an attitude which put his relationship with Elizabeth in the same category as his liaison with Mildred—an attitude which put Elizabeth herself on a level with Mildred. Against this he was bound by some mysterious and undefined code to protest.

"Look here, Conrad, talk as you want, but leave my private affairs out of it. This business of chasing girls may be a great big game to you; but there are people who treat life differently. They have ideals . . ."

"My God, don't I know it!" Conrad broke in rudely. "And what black misery they cause. Wherever there are ideals, you'll find misery."

"How would you know?" Roger asked slyly.

Conrad laid one hand flat on top of the other on his knee with the formal air of one about to make a speech. Roger regretted having asked him the question.

"It's a simple case of cause and effect. Take Mildred and myself, for instance. Neither of us is cursed with ideals, I'm glad to say. So, when we got sick of each other, we were able to part amicably in a civilized fashion. But suppose one of us had had a head full of notions about honour and fidelity, the sacred ties of marriage, the unbreakable vow, and all that nonsense. Why, it would have been hell for both of us, and for our relations too!"

"He's quite right," Roger said quietly, "though he puts it rather pompously."

"Of course I am. If I want your wife and you want mine, we can fix it neatly enough, provided we're civilized; but if we're still barbarians with primitive nonsense in our heads about sacred pledges and vows, then we start clawing each other's hearts out. It's the law of the jungle. All the balyhoo about marriage and womanhood is just surviving magic. Pure superstition, really."

"It's not as simple as that," Howard said. For indeed it all seemed very remote from Elizabeth with her brown eyes and hair and that searching frankness which had turned his own personality upside down.

"As simple as eating porridge," Conrad said, as though wearily impatient with a difficult pupil. "A man's made one way and a woman's made another way. We know what the difference is all about by the time we're eleven years old. And it's all damned good fun, and the more of it the better. But why it should be mixed up with a lot of drivelling taboos that make the world miserable, I don't understand. If we were all really civilized, you'd be able to take a woman to bed quite naturally."

"I don't find anything unnatural about it as it is," Roger said.

"You know what I mean. It would be plain and straightforward, like eating a bar of chocolate."

"Sounds a bit dull," Roger said. "Though I suppose you can have quite a bit of fun peeling the silver paper off."

"As things are, we turn a pleasure into a torment."

"I'd no idea you were so wise, Conrad," Roger said. "I thought you only understood beef-steaks and hors-d'œuvres and that kind of thing. You're quite right. Being civilized is the art of living simply. And this business of sex ought to be the simplest thing of all."

"No one has suggested that it's difficult," Howard said, aware that a good deal of hot air was being generated. "Any fool can tumble a girl."

"But it takes a civilized man to do it simply, without any fuss or spurious sentiment."

"It ought to be like eating a meal," Conrad went on. "It should be done decently and appreciatively." His hands shaped in the air something that might have been a tureen of potatoes. On the other hand it might have been part of the female body. Perhaps it was meant for both. "You mustn't gobble. Neither must you gape and snivel. Above all, you mustn't mix religion up in it."

"In what?" Howard asked. "Eating or wenching?"

"Either. That's the whole point. The approach should be the same in each case. It's nonsense to bind yourself eternally to a steak and kidney pie. And it's nonsense to bind yourself to a woman."

Roger blinked up at Conrad—a look suggestive of increasing inebriation.

"Keeping a hotel has made you into a philosopher, old man. No wonder you didn't get on with Mildred. She was never one to be served up on a plate with a glass of stout."

"She takes men just that little bit too seriously," Conrad admitted. "There's that much idealism about her. Not the goody-goody brand; but the ravenous primitive matriarch. It comes to the same thing in the end. Both types want to eat you up. And it's not civilized."

"It's a gross simplification," Howard said, half amused at Roger's cynical exaggerations and half angry with him for being who he was.

Conrad stood up as if to leave and shrugged his shoulders.

"It's not particularly gross; but it's simplification all right. That's what it's meant to be. You've got to simplify. You've got to live on the surface of life, or you'll take a header into misery. Once you go deep, you're finished. You become either a snivelling sinner or a pasty-faced saint. And it's damned awful to be either."

"I disagree," said Roger. "It's fine being a sinner. Nobody minds that."

Conrad glanced from Roger to Howard.

"Take my tip," he said confidentially. "If you're breaking with Mildred, make it a sharp, clean break. There'll be merry hell if you don't."

The atmosphere was more restful after Conrad's

84

departure. Roger stretched his long legs and watched his suède shoes tapping each other, reflectively.

"I did warn you, you know."

"About what?"

"Falling for a respectable girl. Respectability makes everything very complicated. And then for a girl with some religion too! That's even tougher. It takes six months to effect a decent convincing conversion. Then you have to start from scratch. It's hard going for twelve months."

Although Howard and Roger had for years enjoyed conversation together on this half-cynical, half-flippant level, Howard now began to feel that it jarred. More, he began to feel hypocritical for allowing it. Since his talk with Canon Kirkbride things were different. It was not that his beliefs had changed. Not that at all. But Canon Kirkbride had spoken so frankly and fully with him about his own convictions that Howard felt himself bound in loyalty to speak of religion differently now. Not, of course, as something that he believed in; but as something that was not necessarily stupid and contemptible. As something which a man might take very seriously and yet be neither a fool nor a hypocrite. This represented a deeper inner change than Howard would yet have reckoned with consciously.

"You don't understand even now," he said. "It isn't just a question of keeping Elizabeth happy. You can't treat this business of a Church marriage simply on that level. I thought you could, but you can't. It opens up too many side-issues. It's difficult to explain; but I went to see the parson at St Margaret's about it, and he made me feel like that."

85

Roger whistled quietly. It implied a considerable degree of astonishment.

"Don't mistake me," Howard went on. "The fellow didn't convert me. I don't think he even tried to. But he's a good type, and he's got a brain. And he makes you see that there *is* something in this religion of theirs. It makes you think."

Roger's smooth sloping forehead was suddenly creased in a frown. He stirred edgily.

"You bloody fool. Of course there's something in it. A damned sight too much!"

This surprised Howard. Roger's suavity was suddenly consumed, not in mockery, but in petulant irritation.

"I didn't know you had any use for it," Howard said.

"I don't dabble in it. But I'm not a barbarian."

"Not even a pagan?"

"Look here," Roger said, with exceptional warmth. "These dunderheaded plutocrats like Conrad think the world is just a great fat cake that they can cut in little bits and eat. Your parsons say that it isn't anything of the kind. And they're quite probably right, as you and I know well enough. So what? We're not going to make ourselves miserable about it. That's the difference between us and your parsons."

"But if they're right, then we ought to do something about it."

"If they're right," said Roger, waving his hand impatiently, "that's all the more reason to forget it while we can. We shall have to remember that kind of thing soon enough."

86

It was the first time Howard had ever heard Roger speak, even remotely, of death and the ultimate meaning of things. He was astonished to discover in him this underlying respect for the deeper, the religious view of life. His face, normally very white, the face of a soft-living indoor man, was flushed about the cheekbones, and his right foot performed a rapid little dance of irritation. He lit a cigarette and made an effort to clarify his outburst calmly.

"You've been told already by Conrad in his halfbaked way. You leave that kind of thing alone, or else you go in for it in a big way. You skim the surface or else you dive to the bottom. If you've any sense, you'll skim the surface. Life is too short to spend it chattering about sin."

"What else are we doing most of the time?" Howard asked.

Roger drank and then paused to laugh. Somehow he had recovered his normal poise.

"You've got it bad. In another three weeks you won't be fit company for ordinary decent fellows. They'll get hold of you good and proper, these parsons. They'll whitewash you and take you around to talk to mothers' meetings. 'Mr Howard Prentice, our new lay-reader. Mr Prentice will speak on *My life of sin*. Of special interest to mothers with young daughters.'"

Somehow Howard could not laugh at this. Roger's transition was too abrupt. But he was launched, and he stoked up his own raillery. It provided an escape from the threat of seriousness still hanging menacingly in the air around them.

"'The Church and Vice. Mr Prentice speaks from

personal experience of the wickedness in our midst. Film-strip entitled *See for Yourself* by the Moral Reform Society. Unmarried mothers welcomed. Collection for the Mission to Street-walkers.' "

"All right," Howard said. "I've heard."

But Roger was not to be suppressed. He raised both hands in a gesture of histrionic piety.

" 'My good ladies, would you believe that it is but two months ago that I was myself a lost man? But two months since I sat in a disreputable bar of this our beloved city, listening to the blasphemies of a boon companion—a man given over to all manner of licentiousness, a man whom no woman could meet without a blush?' "

"You flatter yourself," Howard said, and he stood up, having had enough. Roger stood up too, but only in order to make his performance more realistic.

" 'My dear sisters, my dear, dear sisters, I cannot think of this man without sorrow. He stands for ever in my mind as an example of hopes and promises blighted by evil ways. Talented, handsome, gifted with a ready wit and a glib tongue, he wasted himself in undisciplined frivolity and vicious excess. And he boasted of his sins, perverting the language of religion and making a mockery of all that is sacred. No woman was safe in his company. Let us pause and say a silent prayer for his miserable soul. I will give you his address at the conclusion of the meeting.' "

Howard moved off, and Roger followed him up into the street. Howard was displeased, for Roger's mockery seemed to make it even more impossible to think soberly about the impending difficulties. Every possible

88

serious consideration which might be given to the Kirk-bride code was made to appear hypocritical in advance. Not surprisingly, Howard still showed no appreciation of his friend's performance.

"Sorry," Roger said, feeling that his efforts had misfired inexplicably, and trying to compensate with a barrage of heavy irony. "Don't be put out." He touched Howard's shoulder. "Turn your back on the scoffer and the railer. Go and put on sackcloth and ashes. Then marry the good woman and plant the olive branches around your table."

"How can I even think straight, when you make everything so absurd?"

"There," Roger said dramatically. "I sully everything I touch. Forget it."

"I'm doing my best."

Roger stuffed his hands in his overcoat pockets and looked skywards. Another stage gesture.

"I'm a bad influence on you. You must drop me. There's a better self in you, struggling for the purer air."

"Oh, shut up."

"I mean it. I recognize the symptoms. I've seen them before in my more helpless victims. It hurts me as much as it hurts you. I can't meet you now without being reminded of my own depravity."

"You spend a great deal of time reminding me of it yourself."

"The effect of your presence. You're beginning to carry the odour of sanctity about with you."

The irony was so good-natured that, in the end,

Howard could not but be amused: but Roger raised his hands at the sight of Howard's smile.

"Don't laugh. Everything I say is diabolical. Spurn the tempter in me."

"The odd thing is," Howard said, "that you seem to use the right vocabulary."

"Acquired in my infancy; perverted in my maturity. That's the tragedy."

Howard sighed.

"You're impossible, Roger."

"I manage to exist nevertheless."

"I think the trouble is," Howard went on, musing on his friend's peculiar brand of flippancy, "that you haven't enough interests. Why don't you take up golf or politics, or something?"

"Because I'm an ascetic by nature. I shrink from the dissipations of ordinary men. One pursuit is enough for me. I have chosen drink because it doesn't corrupt the moral fibre like politics or games. Drinking is a kind of discipline, provided you are prepared to specialize in it. It concentrates your resources on a single end, and keeps you out of mischief. Without it, I might be in the same danger as you—advertising my soul at street-corners, and shooting a line in kingdom come."

"No danger of that," Howard said, a little riled to be under attack again, however perverse.

"I'm only warning you. All drugs grow on you. That's why it's important to choose an innocent sociable one, like drink. If you go in for religion, you will become unbearable. Putting your nose into other fellows' business, and corrupting girls by whispering

Allelulia, instead of making decent, honest approaches to them in plain English. Many a man has gone to the dogs like that."

"You know," Howard said. "I think you are bringing your own secret fears about yourself to light. That's the psychology of it. You try to be cynical and immoral, but you can't do it. Underneath all your flippancy, you're really attacking hypocrisy all the time. You speak of my being in danger of virtue—but look at yourself. If the parsons got hold of you they'd turn you into a raving saint overnight. You're one of the greatest moralists alive; but too humble to admit it."

Roger laughed heartily; and then took up the theme with zest.

"The moralist of the century. All done on whisky. The Jolly Roger comes clean at last. Book your seats for the opening night at the Harringay Arena. Pharisees not admitted."

"Meantime, watch the traffic," Howard said, as Roger advanced to set foot too soon on a pedestrian crossing. "I'll be seeing you."

"I'll try to get back to earth. Watch yourself too," Roger said, and then dived into the traffic.

"I THINK it was a complete waste of time."

Roland had just given Canon Kirkbride a rather racy account of the evening's parish visiting which he and Julia had done, and that was how he summed it all up. Julia disagreed.

"No, Roland, that's not fair. After all, we met several people. Mrs Badger is a dear; and the others were kind, you know."

"Did we *really* meet them?" Roland asked. "I don't think we did. I know we came face to face with them in the same room. We said words—or rather you did—and they heard them and said other words in reply. But it doesn't follow that we really *met* them in the true sense of the word. For did any of them really receive and understand what you were trying to say? Was there any effective communication? I don't think so. If we're honest, we must admit that we never got into touch with anyone that evening."

"We listened," Julia said, "even if we weren't listened to. That's something, I think."

"It's quite a lot," the canon said.

"It's nothing to the purpose surely," Roland went on. "This is how I see it. Each of them stayed in his own little world and shouted things out to us. And we

—in our different world—heard these cries from the distance and occasionally tried to send out messages in reply. But really it was all one-way traffic. We sat there, patiently receiving. But did we manage to get any message back? No. Our job was about as one-sided as sitting, counting the bleeps from an earth-satellite. And that's why I say it was all a waste of time. We failed. Because we went to talk, not to be talked to—or at least you did."

"Did she?" the canon asked heavily.

"Indeed I didn't," Julia said.

"You were hoping to convert someone, weren't you?"

"My dear Roland," the canon said, "I happen to have led you into scepticism about your scepticism by means of conversation, and for ever after you're going to imagine that evangelism is all talk. I assure you it isn't. Even in your own case it wasn't. My talk may have shifted you from some of your grosser misconceptions, but it wasn't my talk which brought you to God. It was things that people did—two things especially, involving two people. Am I not right?"

Roland smiled in acquiescence.

"Yes. Brother James and Simon Phelps."

"Exactly. They touched you. They showed you the way. Not by shouting anything at you. Not by conducting a great evangelical campaign in your vicinity. But just by dying. Brother James by dying to the world: by turning from the attractions of ambition, property, and family life, and taking monastic vows. Simon Phelps by taking leave of life altogether. I'm afraid often the most fruitful thing we can do is that—one way or another to die."

There was a moment's quiet as this sad truth sank again into Roland's mind. Then Canon Kirkbride shook his head thoughtfully.

"It is perhaps one of our most serious errors to-day," he went on, "to imagine that souls can be won for our Lord chiefly by talk."

Julia looked at Roland with much sympathy in her eyes. Had he perhaps been too drastically deflected?

"In a way Roland is right, Father. Mrs Badger and the others didn't understand what we said. There's an awful gap, which is so hard to cross."

"He *was* right about that," the canon agreed. "But I didn't like his other point. We must not declare something to be a waste of time merely because we cannot ourselves see exactly what it has achieved. That habit reflects a myopic materialism."

"I used the phrase 'waste of time' carelessly perhaps," Roland said in apology. "You know what I mean by it. Simply that Julia's efforts that night didn't ostensibly get anywhere. I'm not saying that we should have done as much good by going to the cinema; but I think that, taking your point of view, as parish priest, we could have spent the evening in some way more likely to help the work of the Church."

"That you cannot say," the canon replied firmly. "It is a very condition of our life on this planet that we cannot at any given time see the full pattern which our immediate actions help to weave. To expect to see it is to claim the prerogative of divinity."

Canon Kirkbride's firmness on what seemed to

Roland to be a very subsidiary issue surprised him. It was not like the canon to labour unimportant points. Rather he was a man who strove to preserve a just sense of proportion. Why then make such a fuss about his trivial comment on the evening's activity? No sane man could have made much of a claim for what they had done that night in Denvers Street.

"Aren't you labouring a rather trivial point, Father?"

Canon Kirkbride removed his glasses, blew on the lenses, and proceeded to rub them clear with a handkerchief.

"Either a thing is worth doing or it is not worth doing. If it is worth doing, and we decide to do it, and we do it to the best of our ability, we must not worry afterwards if we find ourselves personally disappointed in the results. Especially is this the case when we enter upon some undertaking in the name of God himself. For we must believe that God is concerned about efforts made in his service especially, and that he overlooks those efforts. And we must remember this. The fruit God chooses to derive from our efforts may be very different from the fruit we personally hoped to produce. If so, well and good. You will admit, I think, that the fruit God chooses is better than the fruit you would have chosen yourself. And in any case, since you may not even be able to see what this fruit is, you can certainly not pass judgment upon it."

Smiles passed between Julia and Roland as the canon progressed thus in his most tidily socratic manner.

"I still can't imagine that we did anything for those

people last Tuesday." Roland was unconvinced. The canon eyed him significantly.

"But perhaps God did something. Not necessarily for those you visited: maybe for you, the visitors. Perhaps God has now used the occasion to teach you, Roland, that talk can't do everything. Perhaps he has used it to teach Julia that you can't help God by suddenly deciding to do a job for him. But you can be *used* by God, if you are willing, when and how God chooses."

The canon closed his eyes. Was it too much to hope that by just such stages a much better, more demanding way of service might offer itself to Julia?

In the silence Julia's eyes were cast down.

"Father, how did you know what I have been feeling about last Tuesday?"

"I didn't know. Have I hit the nail on the head?"

"Yes, you have. You've said just what I've been telling myself ever since."

"I thought it possible," the canon said quietly. "Spiritual experience repeats itself, you know. Each of us is unique; but we all make the same pilgrimage."

The frankness of Julia's momentary self-revelation made Roland feel small. He looked at her in admiration. She was wearing a plain blue dress, short-sleeved and square-necked, and her hair embraced her cheeks like the habit of a nun. For a moment her grey eyes were wide with candour, and Roland told himself, as he told himself long ago, that she was very beautiful. Hair and cheek met in a long curve. Yet when her lips and eyes came to life in conversation, any hint of the voluptuous was blown to the winds. Roland had an observant eye, and he noted this as remarkable. With other girls it was different. The flow of line and the sheen of texture are touched by the light and shade of movement and, suddenly, tranquillity matures into desirability. Not so with Julia. When she spoke or laughed, desire died away in the dancing of her features; languor was irradiated into gaiety.

Julia, now staring at the canon in some perplexity, said, "Father, you tell us how difficult it is to get in touch with people; and we've seen for ourselves how true that is. But why? Why should it be? The things the Church has to teach—the important things—are simple enough; so simple that children can take them in. Our Lord was born in Bethlehem and the Virgin Mary was his mother. That isn't hard to understand. All the most important things we believe are simple and clear like that. Then why should it be so hard to speak of these things in a way that makes people listen?"

The canon stared into the fire. He knew the answer to this one—or rather, he grasped it, felt it, lived with it. But how frame it in words? How sum up the astonishing fact of the twentieth century's headlong flight from God? How make this flight appear, as in truth it must appear, an aberration almost unparalleled in history for its scope and intensity? How clinch in words—not the fact of contemporary man's rebelliousness (that was easy to do and would scarcely illuminate the total situation)—but the sheer blindness which lay at the back of that rebellion, making is possible, making it inevitable, making it wholesale?

"You see," Julia went on, pressing her bewilderment

97

more heavily upon the canon, "people are not unhelpful. They are kind. They want to do what is right. They are concerned that there should not be cruelty and meanness in the world. Most of them are like that. But . . ." Her sentence trailed off into the perplexity of silence.

"But God doesn't enter into it," Roland said. "They don't know him, as Brother James put it. And it doesn't seem very long ago."

"Let's not embroider the original point just yet," said the canon, who preferred a direct argument to a drifting one. "Why should it be hard to interest people in the Christian Faith? That is our question."

"And a big enough one in all conscience," Roland said.

"Suppose," said the canon, "we are trying to educate a child who has been blind from birth. We shall find it easy to talk to him about the cries of animals and the songs of birds. But how do we explain to him what a star or a sunset is like? I don't know. It's a mystery to me how people teach the blind about things like that. I'm sure it must be fascinating and rewarding work to do. But I'm also sure that it must be strenuous work, making great demands upon the teacher's patience. And I know this too. It's no use talking to blind children as though they could see."

Roland nodded.

"You mean that unbelievers are blind?"

"Without eyes," said the canon, "the child cannot appreciate the visible world. Without an awareness of the spiritual order above and around us, a man cannot take in the truths of our religion."

"And you think it is just as hard to talk to un-believers about the Christian Faith as it is to talk to blind children about the visible world?"

"In one way much harder," said the canon. "And for this reason. The blind child *knows* that through lack of eyesight he is deficient in respect of a whole sphere of human experience. But the modern un-believer has frequently no knowledge that he is defi-cient in respect of a whole sphere of human experience. Try to teach a blind child who refuses to believe that there is such a thing as eyesight. That is something like our difficulty with the unbeliever. He thinks he is a full man. Yet he is totally deficient in a perceptiveness for lack of which he is shut out from the knowledge of God and cut off from the source of life's meaning and true joy." The canon paused a moment on the brink of getting to the core of the matter. "I'm afraid people keep their minds at work in a very limited sphere. Their thinking is pegged down within a seventy-year span of eating and sleeping, getting and spending. They do not allow for the heights above and for the depths beneath the narrow road through time. They do not see man's earthly pilgrimage against the back-ground of a more stable and wholly superior order of being."

"But surely," said Roland, "many of the people out-side the Church—the people we are talking about—surely many of them have got some notion of the supernatural. They believe in a kind of after-life."

"Mere superstition," said the canon decisively. "The picture of an after-life which merely extends indefi-nitely the pattern of our earthly search after comfort

99

and well-being—that is a dreamy superstition. Indeed it turns Christian thinking topsy-turvy. For it constructs in the mind a heavenly life which is little more than an appendage to earthly life. No, true belief relates to a God who is at the centre of creation, at the centre of all that is and has been. But if a man's mind naturally and habitually places man at the centre of things—a centre in relation to which God is on the periphery—then true belief is impossible.

"We all know that our picture of any event, object, or character, is affected by our point of view. A great cathedral has one appearance to a man in the nave, another to a man outside the west door, and another again to an aeroplane pilot above it. There is nothing that looks the same from the inside and from the outside. We see earthly life from the inside. We are involved in it, enclosed in it. Is that view, the man's view, the full and final view? Humanism and atheism say yes. We say no. Before you can profess religious belief, you must be able to conceive of an outside view of human life which is the full and final view, and by comparison with which our human view is partial and incomplete. I'm afraid this is a very *sine qua non* of true religious conviction. Before we can truly believe, worship, and obey, we must mentally place ourselves off-centre in relation to the whole known set-up, and thus leave room for a God.

"You see, as long as we speak of God, we mean a being in relation to whom man is off-centre. But as the contemporary unbeliever and humanist receives our word 'God', he conceives of yet one more 'thing' which is off-centre in relation to man. There you have our dilemma. The unbeliever's mode of thinking ensures that he will not start to believe. It ensures that he will not take in anything we say about the facts of revelation. It thus precludes the possibility of effective communication between us.

"Truths of revelation record the breaking in of the outer supernatural order upon our limited natural world. That, to us, is of their very essence—the thing which makes them what they are. But if the natural world is seen as the totality of things—or even as the dominant sphere of existence—then the notion of the greater breaking in upon it is an absurd impossibility. There is no greater than it to break in upon it. The tragedy is that the word 'God' is used by men who are limited in their thinking in exactly that way. The being this word 'God' connotes is one who clings precariously to the periphery of the known and tried and mastered establishment which is man's universe, like a dog hanging by the teeth to his master's leash and trailing some feet behind him. That is the rôle in which God is cast by those for whom the finite and the human provide all significant values, all final motives and criteria. We must ourselves beware lest, not perhaps in our intellectual life, but in our daily pursuits, desires, and aspirations, we cast God by implication for the same dismal and servile rôle."

To anyone capable of self-criticism, this was a disturbing statement, and therefore it disturbed Roland. He recognized that in this new development of the argument Canon Kirkbride had defined a rigorous criterion by which genuine religious conviction could be tested. He had virtually put it in the form of penetrating questions. Does your religious thinking—does your religious life—posit first and centrally a self established in finitude to whom, from somewhere afar off, a God sends in his tribute of assistance and protection? Or does it posit first and centrally a God enthroned in eternity, on whom each self is hourly dependent for being, breath, and sustenance? Does your God stand like a supernatural lackey, holding over earthly pilgrims the gaudy umbrella of divine philanthropy? Is the eternal Footman stealthily and obsequiously at man's service in the mansions of time? Is he the hanger-on of history?

Or is he, supreme, enthroned, untouchable, God indeed?

Julia was still tussling with the issue which had given birth to this digression.

"I can't follow, Father. That wouldn't matter at all if you were talking about something frightfully up-in-the-air and out-of-the-way. But you're speaking of the way people have to begin to look at things if they are going to believe. That ought to be simple. You say it is simple. Then why must all these words be spilt over it? It's not like you to make difficulties for the fun of it. And you're always warning us about having God-in-the-head instead of . . . well, instead of whatever it is that should be wherever it ought to be."

"My dear Julia," said the canon, smiling, "although I have never been attached to the modern theory that the sexes are in all things equal, nevertheless . . ."

"Now, now," Roland interrupted with mock solemnity.

"Yes?" Julia queried archly, with a contrived air of meekness. "Nevertheless what?"

"Well," the canon went on, becoming quickly serious again, "a ball is a very simple thing; but the mathematics of the sphere is certainly not child's play. That shows you, I think, that very simple things can be difficult to explain and analyse in words."

"Yes," Julia said hastily, "but we're not talking about things that need to be explained mathematically. We're talking about ordinary simple men and women and how they think—and how they ought to think. Now you two would regard me as a simple woman—I can see that in your expressions—so you ought to be able to make it all clear to me."

Canon Kirkbride rubbed his head.

"You talk of being a simple woman. I'm afraid I must be an even simpler man. For I'm quite lost now. What is it that I'm supposed to explain to you simply?"

"How it is that anyone ever gets converted, if it is so difficult as all that to put people in the right way of thinking first?"

"Ah."

Canon Kirkbride sounded, now that the question had been voiced, as though he had expected it all along. He picked up his pipe and his tobacco pouch.

"I think that God very often touches men in their sufferings. I had a case in this parish not so long ago. A man who, as he admitted to me, had never in his whole life entertained a thought of God. His only son died unexpectedly. Soon afterwards a sense of human dependence overwhelmed him. For the first time in his life he pictured a state of existence beyond this, and earthly life began to look brief and shaky by comparison. For the first time he thought of a lasting peace and fulfilment, and earthly achievement and possessions began to look cheap and unsatisfying by comparison. He is a very simple man who could not possibly define his state of mind in words like these. But that is what happened to him, if I interpret him aright. His brain was shaken, at least temporarily, into an awareness of life's transience and contingency, into a dim sense of man's creaturely status. It is a simple development which some shock or some suffering quite often produces. I've seen it before. The tragedy is that it doesn't always last."

"Does it usually touch the springs of religious conviction?" Roland asked.

"In many cases, not for long. But there is always hope that it will leave its mark."

"And that is the meaning of suffering?"

"It is part of the meaning of suffering certainly. I have seen men temporarily shaken out of selfish complacency by the sufferings of others and by their own sufferings. Of course people are sometimes made worse by suffering—embittered, and warped, and sour. That is always a sad thing to see. But I'm bound to admit that, in my experience, many a man has been the better for suffering.

"Think about it in your own case. Certainly I must admit myself that whenever some physical trouble comes to remind me of my age, I tend to pray the more fervently and meditate the more intently. As the trouble passes, the temptation to neglect the things of the spirit grows stronger. I'm afraid we are often at our worst when things go well. Then, when pain or distress shakes us, we turn with new resolution to God. I think this is a natural tendency. It operates within the Christian fold and without. Within the fold suffering puts pressure upon us to be more obedient. Outside the fold suffering puts pressure upon men to abandon the tacit assumption that they are gods and not creatures. We can take the argument so far, if no further. Suffering, in one way or another, tends to bring us down a peg. It reminds us that we are men."

Roland knew well enough that this was true. It was little more than twelve months since he had seen Simon Phelps die of sclerosis at the age of twenty-two. That had marked the turning-point of his own spiritual pilgrimage. It was that which had brought him into the Church—not direct personal suffering, in his case, but the spectacle of another's suffering and his death. Was the spectacle of suffering the same in its effects as suffering itself? He was just on the point of putting this question to Canon Kirkbride when suddenly the answer stared him in the face. It was not that he had merely *watched* Simon's suffering and Mrs Phelp's suffering as a detached observer. He had sympathized with them; he had shared their suffering. For to sympathize was to share. It seemed impertinent—almost irreverent—to say so, for of course his taste of distress, in comparison with theirs, had been as a pinprick to an amputation; but nevertheless, in feeling for them and with them he had accepted a token of their agony.

In the grave silence Canon Kirkbride began to fill his pipe, eyeing his two guests as he did so. He could have wished for less warmth between them—or, at least, for fewer glances of mutual understanding. For these glances were rich in self-commitment; a commitment deeper, no doubt, than open utterance allowed for; a commitment deeper, perhaps, than they intended or were conscious of. The canon lit his pipe with an almost ferocious concentration in his eyes. If Julia Dean were setting out on the road to marriage, then it was the end of a five-year dream. A dream it would have to be accounted, even though backed by much prayer. It was a pity. His ministry had produced so few vocations to the religious life. And here, in Julia, had seemed to be one of the surest, growing before his eyes, and certainly one full of the richest potentialities. She had so much to give, and she gave so generously. All those retreats, those frequent week-day Communions, those visits to the Convent at Norburgh. He had assumed that she was feeling her way.

The canon withdrew his pipe from his mouth and sighed. His mind went back, five years, to that dim January morning when he had that last conversation with Mrs Dean, Julia's mother, one of the devoutest and saintliest souls he had even been privileged to minister to. After a great deal of pain in the later months, it was during the last few days a peaceful death; and what Mrs Dean had said then took on that oracular flavour which we allow to the last utterances of grave-minded folk. He at least could never forget what she said about Julia that cheerless morning. He stood there by her bed and saw through the window a dismal wind-swept sleet plastering itself over the heads and bent backs of men and women trudging to work. The cold was so dank and all-pervasive that, in spite of the electric fire, he felt it eat into his bones as he looked down on Mrs Dean's incongruously peaceful face. Perhaps the sheer discomfort of the physical conditions at this, the dead season of the year, had served to render even death itself that little less unattractive. At any rate Mrs Dean spoke and smiled as one possessed of a great inner calm.

"You know, Father, I've always hoped that one of our children would be called to serve God in some dedicated way. I used to pray that it might be Gregory. But it hasn't turned out like that. He isn't the type for the priesthood, I suppose. I accept that. Perhaps," Mrs Dean smiled faintly, "perhaps I've been too ready to accept it because he isn't my own child . . . but I hope it isn't that. I've always tried to treat him as my own."

"You have done all you could, and should, for him," the canon murmured.

"Well, you can guess what I'm going to say, Father. I hope now that it will be Julia who gets the call. I hope it so deeply. I've prayed very hard. She's a good girl. You must watch her, Father."

And so, faithful to his charge, the canon had not ceased to watch Julia. He had watched with a growing sense of deep obligation, for he conceived it his duty as a priest to pay the maximum attention to such solemn statements as Mrs Dean's. He had watched in the expectation of seeing in Julia's life the gradual realization of her mother's hopes and prayers.

To one person alone had he ever mentioned that he looked for Julia to reveal a vocation. This was Brother James who had gratified him one day by saying, quite spontaneously, that Julia had the look of a dedicated soul, and he wondered whether she might not come to feel a call to the religious life. Canon Kirkbride was delighted. He regarded this as virtually a "sign". He assured Brother James that this was exactly what he looked and prayed for. Whereupon the enthusiasm of the religious had overflowed in the good monk. He saw her vowed and wimpled. There was the light of life-long obedience in her eyes.

And now here was Roland Tay, his eyes caressing her head, fondling her hands, fitfully lingering now on the curve of her cheek, now on a fold in her skirt. Roland, but twelve months a Christian, but six months a communicant, planning to snatch this most precious thing from the fold which had just warmly received him. That was how he saw Julia—a treasure, unblemished and infinitely serviceable, about to be laid humbly and prayerfully, an oblation at God's feet.

Canon Kirkbride suddenly frowned and bit his bottom lip. God forgive me, he said to himself. She is no thing at my disposal. Nor is he a thing. And I have no infallibility. It is God's will, God's will, not mine . . . And yet, and yet, the call seemed to be there: and we have prayed so hard.

There was a tap on the door.

"Come in."

The canon's expression suggested that he recognized the tap.

It was Gregory.

"I barged in," he said apologetically. "I think Mrs Cogan must be deaf."

"She's out," the canon explained.

"Oh. Well, I could have walked off with all your silver and valuables without the slightest difficulty."

"Other than that of finding any," the canon said.

"I suppose you haven't seen the evening paper?"

Gregory's hand went to the inside pocket of his overcoat.

"No."

"I thought not. That's why I'm here."

"Is it interesting?" Roland asked.

"To all of you."

Gregory produced a copy of the *Delphwick Evening Mercury* and handed it to the canon. Julia and Roland jumped up and went to lean over him from either side.

"The price of becoming public figures," Gregory said. "It's heavy."

The three of them stared, their eyes glued to the print. Their names jumped out towards each of them from the middle of a double column. Mr Niblett had done his worst.

NIBBLINGS
BY GNAT

Who says the Church is asleep? Who says Church people are out of touch with their fellow-citizens? Who says they are up in the clouds and don't care?

Not me for one. And not the Rev. M. Kirkbride, rector of St Margaret's, Delphwick. He knows they *do* care. And every man-jack in his parish in going to know it too. For this go-ahead parson (M.A. Oxon., and formerly Secretary of the Delphwick Social Union) has stirred up his Church folk to a real job of parish evangelism. Not a stunt this time.

Nothing fancy. No street-corner singing. No brass band. But solid, door-to-door work. Honest, down-to-earth, man-to-man stuff. It's the personal touch all right, and if I know the people of Delphwick (if Gnat the Nibbler knows them, folks!), it's going to stir some of them up to some pretty hard thinking.

Picture Gnat at his fireside on a drab October evening, typing out his ration of Nibblings, and racking his brains what to say, when a live story walks in at the door.

Let me introduce you, folks. Dark, square-shouldered, day-time schoolmaster Mr Roland Tay (Old Delphwegians don't need to ask *which* school!) and petite, honey-blonde Miss Julia Dean, daughter of a prominent Delphwick citizen. They weren't trying to beg anything. And they weren't trying to sell me anything—except a dose of spiritual tonic to do me good.

These young Church-members are taking their religion seriously. They're taking it with them. And they're not taking it home. They're taking it to the fellow next door; and then to the fellow behind the door after that. If that isn't good Samaritanism, then I'll eat my next week's nibblings. Good luck to them! And to far-sighted, one-time rugger-blue Reverend Kirkbride (M.A. Oxon., and formerly Secretary of the Delphwick Social Union). If St Margaret's isn't packed to the doors in a few weeks' time, then it ought to be.

Julia and Roland laughed a good deal, both rather more forcefully than mere amusement warranted, for each was a little embarrassed to see their two names linked like this in print.

Canon Kirkbride did not even smile—at least not for long. His roving eye had fallen upon another familiar name at the bottom of a corner column. There was a brief list of Divorce cases due to be heard at the next sessions in Frond. It was one of these which caught his eye.

Conrad Spruice . . . Mildred Spruice . . . co-respondent, Howard Prentice, Fenhope House, Bevale, Delphwick.

6

THE EDITION of the *Delphwick Evening Mercury* which caused such a stir at the rectory produced the utmost distress in the home of the Lyte family. Elizabeth was badly shaken. When Howard called her on the phone she refused to speak to him. She sent a message to the effect that he must leave her alone: she must have time to think. Mr Lyte, however, assured her in no uncertain terms that, on his part, no time at all was required for thought. The engagement must be terminated. Already he felt that he had been personally affronted. Prentice was a thoroughly bad lot. If he couldn't leave other people's wives alone before he was married, how could they trust him to do so after he was married? Mr Lyte had no intention of watching Elizabeth made miserable for life. It was better that she should suffer a bit now than be humiliated later.

Elizabeth's father was not a man to speak without acting. He sent word to Prentice that, though of course Elizabeth must speak for herself in the matter of their engagement, he himself was now firmly determined not to give his permission for them to marry. Since Elizabeth was only nineteen, her father's word was, for the present, decisive.

But there were others in the family who were less

eager to throw an impending marriage overboard on the spur of the moment. Mrs Lyte, a rather more sensitive person than her husband, felt that he was acting precipitately, and gently suggested that, in this matter, it was the business of everyone to wait upon the feelings and decisions of Elizabeth herself. And Miss Prynne, her maiden sister, who was not unaccustomed to being at loggerheads with both husband and wife, assured them that they would make themselves ridiculous by urging any kind of change whatever in the affair. She could not for the life of her see why Howard's very ordinary escapade should be allowed to put everyone into such a pother. What century did they think they were living in? This was a question frequently put by Aunt Enid in the heat of altercation. She affected a modernity of outlook and a progressiveness in her views which often shocked those about her. To Mrs Lyte this strain in her sister was a cause of some chagrin. Mr Lyte regarded it indulgently as his sister-in-law's great psychological compensation for enforced spinsterhood.

Elizabeth felt inwardly that her father was right, though she gave a very different account of things to herself than ever came to light in conversation with him. For indeed what she felt most sorely was the fact that Howard had kept this business to himself. The fact that he had had so much to hide during the eighteen months in which they had been together could not but suggest an ominous untrustworthiness. If this affair with Mrs Spruice were something over and done with, why had he not confided in her about it? She told herself now that, had he done so, she would have been prepared to forgive. But perhaps the affair was not over and done with. Perhaps it had been going on through the last few months, interwoven with all those meetings and partings in which she had shared. Was it possible—when everything between them had seemed so fresh and frank, so unmatched, so uncontrived? Even now she found it impossible to believe the worst. She knew Howard well enough, she thought, to be able to distinguish between what might be in character and what must be quite out of character. Or did she? She would have said so before to-day. But after to-day?

She buried her face in her hands, sitting there on the edge of her bed with Howard's photograph before her on the dressing-table. It was easy to imagine him led into impetuous entanglements. He was that kind. He didn't wait. He spoke first and thought afterwards. But he wasn't a man to carry on a calculated deception. Surely not that. Recklessness, thoughtlessness, self-indulgence, even vanity—these were within the conceivable range of his defects: but duplicity, no. She would not believe that he had been living a lie.

And yet he had hidden so much. There could be no doubt about that. And, in hiding so much, he had denied her so much. Denied her the opportunity to forgive and comfort, to overlook the lapses, to share the regrets. If there *were* any regrets; if he *did* regret. Surely it must be that he did. It was unthinkable that it should be otherwise. She prayed God that it should not be otherwise. Prayed that illogical, unchronological prayer that all believers sometimes—and, by the logic and chronology of eternity, correctly—pray. That prayer that the past should have been thus and not other. Oh God, may it be that Howard was remorseful for this; was not deceiving me; was not laughing at me. Oh God, in thy eternal now, let it not be that yesterday he laughed at me.

It was in revulsion from discordant voices at home that, a couple of days later, Elizabeth called at the rectory, thus bringing to Canon Kirkbride the first personal encounter with a problem which soon others were to add to and complicate. Many hours of hard thinking and praying in the life of Canon Kirkbride took their character and impulse indirectly from that brief, heated liaison between Howard Prentice and Mildred Spruice. The canon, who loved to trace, where he could, the curious ways of Providence, was oddly moved to think how the connection ran between the weakness of a woman he did not know and the prayers of a priest she had never heard of.

Although she had been nervously apprehensive about going to see the canon, Elizabeth quickly felt at home with him. Seated before his study fire, she was steadied by her very surroundings. These exercised a tranquillizing influence. The Lyte home was just that degree too garish: the patterned carpets shouted at the patterned wall-papers, and the wall-papers screamed at the chair-covers. And there was almost always someone talking: quite often with the radio on as a background. A quiet room in a quiet house, a room that is quietly inhabited —worked in, prayed in—has its own soothing quality. Canon Kirkbride's study, with its dark oak and mono-chrome furnishings, with its book-lined walls and its image-laden mantelpiece, tranquillized by its very differentness. Tranquillized by being personal and all of a piece, expressive of a character not restless and a purpose not trivial.

Anyway the canon himself was a living tranquillizer. Jerky, poiseless personalities, whose thought and talk were all jets and spurts, often fizzled out into sterile silence in the alien calm of his proximity. To noisy, assertive people his company would be like a cavern in which, on entering, they suddenly heard their own voices, bare and exposed, and fell awesomely silent. To the insensitive he was a breakwater: to the sensitive a harbour.

"We can't think of marrying as long as I'm under age. Daddy is quite firm about that. He says I must decide myself about the engagement." Elizabeth fingered her ring sadly. "It's awfully hard. Whatever am I to do?"

She looked at the canon. Her brown hair was parted unmodishly down the middle and swept back loosely over each ear. Her eyes were wide, her lips tight and sad. One of those appealing faces which, from whatever angle you saw it, always seemed to be looking upwards at you.

"What do *you* yourself think you ought to do?" the canon asked.

Elizabeth's eyes fell and she faltered.

"Would you understand if I said that I feel a kind of loyalty that is somehow all the more needed because . . . because of this?"

The canon nodded gravely.

"I certainly understand. It is very right that you should feel that. But questions of loyalty can be very difficult. There is more than one loyalty involved here."

"Yes, I know." Elizabeth spoke on a note of resigned finality. "I've thought about that. There's Daddy too. He says I'm to choose: but I know what he thinks."

"That you ought to break the engagement?"

Elizabeth nodded quickly, as though she could not trust herself to speak. Then, after a pause, she said,

"Something tells me he's right. But there's something else inside me that makes me feel it would be mean—a sort of horrible let-down."

At this point Canon Kirkbride arrived at what he needed to know first of all. He now realized that, when Elizabeth asked his advice, she was not merely seeking corroboration of some course already inwardly chosen. It was clear that she really did want help; that she really was uncertain. And her very uncertainly was, in the canon's eyes, strong evidence that the brake ought to be applied. After all, a girl of nineteen doesn't need any outside encouragement to proceed with an engagement if all is as it should be between the partners.

"I think this is the first thing that needs to be said. An engagement is a promise to marry. It puts you in the position, quite openly and firmly, of being the future wife of the man you are engaged to. Do you still feel that you will become Howard's wife? Are you sure that you want to stand before your parents and friends and acquaintances as his future wife? That is what you are bound to by your engagement."

Elizabeth lowered her eyes and stared at the carpet. Put to her like this, the issue became, not clearer, but more acutely questionable. Not because she didn't know the answer to the canon's question: but because she did know the answer. Without any shadow of doubt she did not at this juncture want to stand before the world as Howard Prentice's future wife. She did not even want to stand before Howard Prentice as his future wife. On the contrary she wanted him, at the very least, to feel acutely unsure of her. But not wanting was one thing; and duty was another thing. Perhaps her desire to keep herself clear of a rather squalid and sordid business was an instance of that very meanness and disloyalty of which she had already spoken. Perhaps this desire was something to be resisted. That was one thread in her thinking—a slightly dramatic urge, always latent in a girl of her age, to martyr herself. And the other thread was a more practical and prudent one. To break an engagement is not generally regarded as throwing a man into a state of healthy uncertainty. On the contrary, it puts him into a condition of certainty. It is final and, generally speaking, irrevocable. The break ought not to be lightly made.

She looked up at the canon.

"I don't want to be pointed at any more as Howard's future wife. But wanting isn't everything."

"It isn't, by any means," the canon said decisively. "But this happens to be one of those cases where wanting is pretty crucial." He looked at her hard. "God has made us what we are in this respect. You cannot pledge yourself to be the mother of a man's children on the strength of a feeling that it might be mean to say no."

The canon put the case strongly for he was convinced that moral pressure was needed here—if only in order to bring to light the power of the emotional resistance to it. But Elizabeth only shook her head sadly.

"You're like Daddy. You've made up your mind that Howard is a bad man."

"No, no." The canon spoke firmly but gently. "I haven't made up my mind. I'm allowing you to make it up for me. You're the only person who can do so in this case."

Elizabeth smiled. It was her first smile of the evening.

"You mean that what you say is only what you think I am thinking myself—deep down?"

The canon replied very softly.

"I am trying to interpret you to yourself."

"Yes. I see. I believe you are doing that. And I suppose I don't want it really. I don't want to face myself."

"We are rarely prepared to face ourselves," the canon said.

Elizabeth received this in silence. Then, after a few moments, she tried to turn Canon Kirkbride's thoughts in a different direction.

"Father, do you think he's so very bad?"

"Why should you expect me to?"

"Because you don't say anything about him—to make it seem less awful."

"No excuses?"

Elizabeth frowned.

"No sympathy—for him," she said.

The canon put his hand to his forehead and momentarily closed his eyes.

"Elizabeth, I prepared you for Confirmation. As a priest, I have a certain responsibility in relation to you. And I am faced with the possibility—we will call it nothing more than that—the possibility that I may be asked to administer the sacrament of Holy Matrimony, binding you in the name of God for the rest of your days to a man of whom I do not know a great deal. But I know rather more to-day than I knew a month ago. Can you expect me to plead on his behalf? Can you expect me to be eager to join you to him in this mysterious sacramental relationship—which is so total in its scope, embracing mind and body, and life-long?"

Elizabeth hung her head and did not speak.

"Read the solemn words of the marriage service," the canon went on, "and then ask yourself what kind of questions I must ask myself before uttering them over two fellow-creatures with my back to God's altar. Must I not, at the very least, be free from grave doubts over the capacity of either party to be faithful to his pledges?"

Elizabeth was still silent.

"You see what I mean?" the canon pressed.

"I think you're right," Elizabeth said quietly, and it sounded tentative, reluctant. "It was a horrible shock at first, and I didn't want to believe it. But not wanting to believe it was really not wanting to be let down. I mean, I was more hurt for myself than for him. That's what I came to see, bit by bit. I didn't want him to have been so deceptive because I couldn't bear to think I was one to have been so tricked. And then, when all this came to me clearly, I felt horribly selfish. To have been thinking about myself all the time, and wanting to be well away from anything unpleasant and distasteful. I began to think I ought to have been thinking more about him. So then I wondered whether I ought perhaps to go through with everything just the same, to try to do something for him the way a girl can."

It was clearer to the canon now.

"If Howard had suddenly been injured, or maimed, through no fault of his own, then there would have been the call for that kind of heroism. But here?" The canon shook his head. "I just don't know. It might be such a case. It *could* be. But the chances are so slight. It's so unlikely. You mustn't think yourself into that kind of sacrifice. For those who feel the call to sacrifice themselves, there are proper establishments, you know."

Elizabeth smiled for the second time. The momentary image of herself as a nun was as amusing as it was novel. Then she became grave again.

"We have to forgive."

She lingered on the words, seeming to ask, what does that mean in a case like this?

"We have to forgive those who seek our forgiveness, those who are truly penitent. It is impossible to forgive a man who does not sincerely regret the offence he has committed. That is true by the very nature of the act of forgiving, which involves two persons, a forgiver and a penitent. In that sense, forgiving is like giving. You cannot give unless there is someone ready and willing to receive. It takes a recipient to transform a man and his money into a giver and a gift. In the same way it takes a penitent to transform a man and his mercy into a forgiver and forgiveness. You cannot forgive intransitively. You can only forgive a certain penitent a certain offence."

"But if he is really sorry, surely we must forgive him completely."

Canon Kirkbride pursed his lips. How say what must be said, without hurting?

"Completely?" He dwelt on the word as though it were highly questionable. "We can forgive only what is in our power to forgive. You can forgive an offence only in so far as it is an offence against yourself. In so far as it is an offence against another, or against society, you personally cannot forgive it. To forgive an offence is to say of that offence, 'It shall be as though it never occurred.' If a man injures you, you alone can say that of the injury. But if a man injures another woman, you have no right at all to say, 'It shall be as though the offence had never been committed.'"

"I see," Elizabeth said in a tone which suggested that she barely saw.

"In plain words, you can forgive Howard for deceiving you. But you cannot forgive him for deceiving Mr Spruice."

"Surely we ought to feel forgiving towards everyone, whatever they have done."

The canon shook his head gravely.

"Forgiveness is not an attitude: it is an action. It is not a state of mind or an emotion which we can assume without reference to the behaviour and intentions of others. To forgive is to act decisively in a concrete situation. And the situation must be such as to allow of the act. I cannot walk the streets, diffusing a vague forgiveness upon passing rogues and hypocrites as a lamp sheds light and warmth indiscriminately. Of course we must always, and in all situations, be prepared to forgive—that which is in our power to forgive."

"And that is very little."

"Often very little."

"Still we must do it without reserve, without holding anything back. You see what I'm thinking of, Father. We have to forget as well as forgive."

Once more the canon's furrowed brow suggested a latent disagreement.

"It is important not to be self-indulgently sentimental at other people's expense. Suppose I have a son who turns out to be a bad lot. He swindles a poor old widow out of her life's savings and squanders the money. Then he comes back home in remorse. It is not my business to say, 'I shall forgive and forget the whole thing,' at the very moment when perhaps the widow is suffering acutely from poverty. It may give me a very nice, cosy feeling inside to say that kind of thing, while someone else is paying the price. It may even make me feel, quite falsely, a very unselfish, merciful, and benevolent type. Most tragic of all, I may even believe that I am being especially charitable and especially Christian by talking and feeling like that. But it would be the most shocking hypocrisy. Talk and feeling of that kind cost nothing: but true charity is always costly."

"You make it sound dreadfully hard," Elizabeth said. "And I've always thought of the gentle, easy people as the ones who are forgiving . . ."

"Who do forgive," the canon corrected. "No doubt it is true that they often do."

"But now you make me think that it's perhaps the

123

easy-going people who are too quick to forget. And I suppose I'm easy-going myself."

The canon lifted his hand reassuringly.

"Elizabeth, I don't imagine you've often found yourself in the kind of position I've been speaking of. Perhaps now you are in just such a position for the first time in your life. That's why I'm trying to help, and to make things clear. When you are in the middle of an awkward situation yourself, it's often very hard to see it clearly, as an outsider would see it. Feelings and notions and sentiments, some of them sound and healthy, some of them not so sound, weave a pattern of confusion inside us. And it is so easy for the worse motive or impulse to appear the better. We have to check our more indulgent impulses especially—even when the indulgence is directed towards another.

"This business of forgiving and forgetting has somehow to be thought about coolly in the light of reason —and in the even fiercer light of that charity which never allows us to purchase sentimental complacency or self-congratulation for ourselves or for our friends at the price of suffering unalleviated elsewhere. You see, you may forgive a man his offence against you, yet you cannot obliterate the continuing results of that offence still present with you. You may forgive a man who has cut your arm off; but that will not restore your arm and enable you to play the piano as you did before you lost it. A man who has set fire to a mansion may perhaps repent and gain forgiveness from the owner. But this act of forgiveness will not magically restore the ancient building. Even after an offence has been forgiven, it may still take years of toil and effort, brainpower and brawnpower, to cancel out the ill effects of that offence. The owner of the mansion might reasonably and charitably forgive the penitent incendiary. But he could not in reason forget that the house had been destroyed. He could not in reason begin to behave as though the ancient building still existed. To forgive magnanimously is fine and noble. But to sleep under the shelter of a non-existent roof is insanity."

At this moment, as the atmosphere was heavy with the weight of the canon's wisdom, there was a knock on the door, and Mrs Cogan came in.

"Two ladies to see you, Father." She looked meaningfully at Elizabeth. "Mrs Lyte and Miss Prynne. They say it's very urgent. Shall I show them in?"

The canon did not hesitate.

"Show them in, Mrs Cogan, certainly."

Nevertheless he thought the visit odd, to say the least. And the way Elizabeth's hand went to her mouth suggested that she was equally unprepared.

She was. But not quite so mystified as the canon. For, having heard several arguments of late on the subject of what ought and what ought not to be done in relation to what really were her own private affairs, Elizabeth guessed that her mother and her aunt had followed her to the rectory to try to prevent something from happening that had already happened. And Aunt Enid, no doubt, was the moving spirit.

The two ladies were ushered in, Mrs Lyte all roundness and smoothness, with her always glinting yet gentle eyes and her complexion like polished soap. Aunt Enid straight-backed, erect, pencil-like, with her dark, expressionless eyes and ever-moving lips.

"Good evening," Aunt Enid said, coming in first.

"Good evening, Father," Mrs Lyte said.

"We thought you were here," Aunt Enid said at Elizabeth, as though Elizabeth had no right to be here, and as though the tracing of her constituted a by no means negligible piece of detective work.

The canon seated the ladies as comfortably as he could. It was not often that his study held three at once. He looked from one to another, wondering what exactly had brought them.

In fact two entirely different motives had operated to unite them on a single practical course of action, namely, to visit Canon Kirkbride and prevent him from further influencing Elizabeth to make a rash decision and break off the engagement. Mrs Lyte's motive was the very genuine fear lest her husband's firmness might hustle Elizabeth into a hasty action likely to be regretted later on. She felt that if the canon, as was likely, asserted the full weight of his moral authority to corroborate her husband's advice, then Elizabeth might well be swayed against her own sounder inclinations. Mrs Lyte was a woman of principle. She would have been only too glad to see Elizabeth, of her own volition, break permanently with Howard Prentice. But she was also a very tender-hearted mother; and she felt it necessary to exert the utmost resistance against pressures upon her daughter. Elizabeth's decision must be her own and not somebody else's. Thus her immediate mission coincided oddly with that of her sister Enid, whose heart burned to assert the freedoms of Atomic Age Morality against the dying ethics of Victorian social servitude. Aunt Enid addressed the canon aggressively.

"We have come to make sure that Elizabeth is not urged to do anything unworthy."

"Anything unworthy?" The canon blinked.

"Anything disloyal to Mr Prentice," Aunt Enid explained, "and therefore unworthy of the girl who has agreed to marry him."

Elizabeth who, on her aunt's entry, had begun to prepare herself mentally to subside into that agony of embarrassment into which her aunt's public performances so often plunged her, lowered her head in uncomfortable silence.

Mrs Lyte smiled her sweetest, roundest smile.

"I do want to be sure, Father, that Elizabeth is allowed to make her own decision."

"You are quite right," the canon said quickly.

"It is, after all, a matter of principle," Aunt Enid went on; and there was a bite in her voice. "It would be quite shameful for a girl to run away from a man when he needs her support most. Shameful and cowardly."

The canon refused to be drawn.

"Do you not agree, Rector," Aunt Enid pressed remorselessly, "that we must have no truck with shameful and cowardly behaviour of that kind?"

The canon hesitated. Was it worth while to embark upon a preliminary dissection of these provocations?

"If I were to concur in your generalizations, Miss Prynne, it would not imply that I believed them relevant to any situation before us to-night."

Aunt Enid was not content to agree to differ. She

was out for blood. As an avid reader of certain progressive and rationalistic journals, she imbibed week by week large doses of that legendary lore about the anachronistic idiocy of things Christian which occupies a place among the more comic superstitions of the sophisticated middle-class. Columnists who make you boil over about bishops every Friday at breakfast time are all very well, but, if you happen to be one of those numerous persons who never meet a bishop to be boiled over upon, then the cumulative effect of this early morning fare over some months is apt to be something like a cross between frustration-neurosis and acute indigestion. Thus, though the anti-Christian journalist's sneers about the Church and her peculiar ways are normally a source of good healthy fun to Christians themselves; in charity they have to bear in mind that these same sneers are apt to cause considerable pain to their repressed and unbelieving fellow-creatures.

Canon Kirkbride, who understood at least something of Miss Prynne's agonizing need to bait him whenever they encountered each other, tried to preserve the proper compassion called out by those who suffer through their own blindness and ignorance.

"It would be wrong," Aunt Enid said with some heat, "it would be immoral to separate Elizabeth from her fiancé merely because he happens to have enlightened views about relations between the sexes."

"I was not aware that Mr Prentice's views were at issue," the canon said. "I understood that it was his actions which have proved disturbing."

"The actions are the product of the views," Aunt Enid insisted. "They are the expression of the views.

Mr Prentice has the courage to express his fearlessly. It is the hypocrite who dare not express his views in action. Mr Prentice has a sincerity which we must surely all admire."

Canon Kirkbride closed his eyes. Immoral, enlightened, courage, sincerity. Every word Aunt Enid uttered was sufficiently misused to make it worthless as a counter to be employed in rational interchange. Where was the link to be found, the bridge over which he and she might communicate? The bridge which could carry some kind of light mental traffic between those who called Howard Prentice's offence adultery and those who called it a sincere and courageous expression of enlightened views?

"I don't think we need argue these things here, Enid," Mrs Lyte said, herself acutely aware of the distance between her sister and the canon.

"Every time and every place is fit for plain speaking," Aunt Enid replied.

The canon's eyes twinkled.

"Now there I must disagree. There are some times and places where plainness would be rather vulgar and in bad taste. Occasions when ceremony is called for. Let's say a Coronation."

The good-humour missed fire. Aunt Enid shook herself irritably, scornfully, as though her grave utterance had been cheapened by the canon's flippancy.

"Mummy," Elizabeth said quietly. "There's no need for any fuss. I've made up my mind."

"Oh!" Aunt Enid drew her shoulders back and raised her voice as though what she heard were totally unexpected.

Elizabeth did not speak. She raised her left arm and spread out her hand. The engagement ring had been removed.

Mrs Lyte shook her head with a sad smile.

"I did hope you would think carefully for a little while, before saying anything final."

"So?" said Aunt Enid.

"It's my own decision," Elizabeth said quietly.

Aunt Enid turned on the canon.

"It is what I expected. That is the fruit of your Christian teaching." She spat the words out. "Suffering, and meanness and disloyalty."

"Enid, really!" Mrs Lyte protested. But it was useless. Her sister was now well launched.

"In my own life I have seen it time and time again. You Christians hate human happiness. When you see it, you try to destroy it."

"Aunt Enid, that's quite unfair. Father Kirkbride has done his very best to help me."

Elizabeth interrupted in vain. The lid was off, and the brew compounded of gobbetts from months of anti-clerical journalism boiled over on the rector's head.

"You hate everything that is really human. You hate happiness. You hate sex. You worship a God who detests sex."

"We worship the God who invented it," the canon said calmly. "And we should be the last people to cast a slur upon his inventions."

This rejoinder, which was logically unassailable, goaded Aunt Enid to shift her ground.

"Whatever he is," she said, "you turn him into a God of cruelty."

"He is a God of love and self-sacrifice," the canon said. "It is true that we tend to forget."

"Love!" said Aunt Enid scornfully, pointing at Elizabeth. "And that is how you show it! You preach love and forbid people to marry. You treat re-married divorcees as outcasts. How can you preach love and yet refuse to forgive?"

Forgiveness again. The canon's eyes met Elizabeth's, understandingly.

"The Church never refuses forgiveness to the penitent, Miss Prynne."

"You refuse it to divorcees."

"One step at a time." Canon Kirkbride spoke in patient, measured tones. "Let us suppose that you had stolen something—a dog perhaps."

"It's unthinkable. Anyway I hate dogs."

Elizabeth too felt that the hypothesis was infelicitous, but the canon persisted.

"Let us suppose it for the sake of argument. Now what must you do if you wish to be forgiven? Of course, you must feel sorry for your theft. But could God—or could the dog's owner—forgive you the sin if you said you felt sorry and yet hung on to the dog? No. That wouldn't be true sorrow or true penitence. If you are truly penitent, you restore what you have stolen to its rightful owner. It's no use saying, 'But I love this dog. I value its company above any other happiness. And it is devoted to me. It came away with me eagerly and shows no inclination to return to its former master.' You see what I mean? When a man steals another man's wife, the case is in some respects the same."

"It's utterly different." Miss Prynne was outraged.

131

"Wives are not men's possessions. Women are not like animals."

"I didn't mean that at all. Put it the other way round, if you like. Say a woman has stolen another woman's husband. It comes to the same thing. In order to be forgiven, you must repent fully. And repentance means that you make restitution for the wrong you have done. Now how can a man or a woman make restitution for taking the spouse of another? How can they make restitution for breaking a marriage vow? Only by returning to their former state. That's the only way. We don't need religion to tell us that. Logic itself makes the point plain. You see, it isn't that the Church refuses to forgive. It's that sinners refuse to repent."

"The law supports them."

"True," said the canon. "The law gives official civic status to the sinner's refusal to repent. It formally registers and licenses that refusal by an agreement which it is pleased to call 'marriage'. But that doesn't deceive anyone who can think straight. The fundamental situation remains unchanged. Suppose parliament were to enact comparable legislation in another field. Suppose it were to arrange that, by appearing before a theft tribunal, a thief could be legally endowed with the goods he had stolen. From that point the thief would become a respectable law-abiding citizen again. But I'm afraid the Church would have to stick to her rather old-fashioned view that the theft remained a sin; and that the thief could not be forgiven unless he restored what he had stolen."

"The Church has no right to speak against the law. Since marriage can be legally dissolved, the marriage vow can be cancelled out. You are speaking of honest law-abiding citizens as though they were criminals."

"Sinners," said the canon, "not criminals."

"It's the same thing."

"No, there's a world of difference. But one point at a time. The ruling that the marriage vow is indissoluble is now, of course, only the ruling of the Church. It applies therefore to her members. You will surely agree that the Church has the right, like any society, to make its own rules for its own members. Generally speaking, they accept those rules loyally. If you think those rules are wrong, well and good. But you must not expect the Church to alter her rules to suit the ideas of people who do not belong to her flock."

There was a momentary silence during which both Mrs Lyte and Elizabeth fervently hoped that Aunt Enid had at last decided to withdraw from the dispute. But they were soon disappointed. Aunt Enid had a persistence on this subject especially which had often astonished those she lived with, not least Mr Lyte, who had frequently expressed to his wife his surprise that a respectable middle-aged spinster should betray such a passionate sympathy with the plight of the promiscuous and the adulterous. Mr Lyte even hinted that there was something heroic about her determination to champion the cause of those whose misfortunes she was never likely to share. He had known before spinsters who begrudged wives their husbands, and more who begrudged mistresses their lovers. But here was a woman who fought doughtily for plurality in a sphere of activity where she was by nature condemned to be a non-starter.

133

"It is Church men and women that I speak of. You refuse to forgive them their lapses."

Canon Kirkbride started again, patient as ever.

"The Church will always forgive the penitent adulterer. But she cannot pretend that her own rules do not exist. Let me explain what rules are and how they affect people. Suppose you are playing cricket. You are batting, and your fellow batsman runs you out. You lose your temper with him, and curse him to his face as you leave the crease. In that case you commit the sin of uncharity. But you haven't broken any rules of the game. The game itself is not upset by your sin. It continues on its proper course. After the match, perhaps, you may put things right by apologizing to your team-mate, and the injury is forgiven. But now suppose, while you are batting, you receive a straight ball in your hand, instead of on the bat, and throw it back to the bowler. There may well be nothing sinful in that. It depends upon the motive. But it is against the rules of the game. The game cannot continue as though nothing untoward had happened. You cannot be allowed to play at all if you persist in doing that kind of thing. Indeed you *ceased* to play cricket the very moment you broke the rule. What you did was not cricket. Of course it's not an exact parallel, but in a similar way divorce is against the rules so far as the Church is concerned. Church men and women do not treat marriage as dissoluble. It isn't Churchmanship!"

Although Miss Prynne was listening less restlessly now, Elizabeth doubted whether the canon's analogies would cut much ice with her. It seemed to Elizabeth as unlikely that her aunt would find herself involved in controversy over a breach of rules at the wicket, as it was that she might be caught red-handed in possession of someone else's dog. But the rector's point seemed to have ended the altercation, for Aunt Enid fell silent.

Then it was that everyone began to feel slightly abashed at the heat of the argument now dying. Elizabeth saw her aunt's features suddenly become still and sad, and she felt ashamed that she had so recently been ashamed of her. To Mrs Lyte, the whole episode was one more instance of her own failure to run things as they should be run. For indeed Aunt Enid had for so long treated her as one who arranged and organized everything incompetently that she had begun to succumb to the propaganda and to believe herself a greater fumbler than she was. Aunt Enid herself, now that her brief outburst of bitterness was spent, began to wonder whether perhaps Canon Kirkbride, being a rare exception, was after all not a characteristic representative of that ecclesiastical breed whose inanities she found frequently held up to scorn in the literature she devoured. He was utterly wrong of course. But he could think.

Meantime Canon Kirkbride sensed acutely the double tragedy of Aunt Enid's personality. The sadness it caused others and the sadness it brought upon herself. It must be hard for the Lytes to have her daily in their household, always by her bitter blend of scepticism and sentimentality wearing away the bloom from the finer feelings of those she lived with. He could picture the hourly strain of having her alien notions and attitudes as a constituent element of the very fabric of their home life. And he marvelled at the charity of Mrs Lyte and Elizabeth, who clearly treated her with the maximum forbearance. Yet, beyond and deeper than his sympathy for these two, was his feeling for Aunt Enid herself. He had seen enough of life to know the suffering of those who are at odds with their own souls and at odds with creation—those to whom nature has been so sparing in her gifts of attractiveness, good-humour, and spontaneous delight. He could see now on Aunt Enid's lined forehead the perplexity of the unlovable soul. Her very burdensomeness to others cried out for compassion. To have an alien presence about was always uncomfortable, unhappy: but to *be* an alien presence, that was bitterness near to despair. She demanded the love that all lost things demand; given against the grain of inclination, given even in the teeth of hostility.

The Canon was deeply anxious to get in touch with Miss Prynne; but he knew that she was of a type the most difficult in the world to get into touch with. Argument would get nowhere, he felt. For argument was the medium she had chosen as the instrument of her protest against the society which made of her a supernumerary. Argument was, by sheer habit, the established vehicle of her bitterness. When she attacked the Christian position, the canon felt bound to reply to her challenge, partly for the sake of the truth itself, partly for the sake of onlookers like Elizabeth and Mrs Lyte, to whom it was his duty to make clear where Aunt Enid's reasoning was at fault. But in doing so, he never cherished the illusion that he was helping Aunt Enid herself much. Rather he feared all the time that he was perhaps pushing her further into twisted hostility against Christian orthodoxy. That was why he responded reluctantly to her wild statements and made no attempt to force the controversial pace.

At this point it seemed therefore that the little gathering might break up without any further heated discussion. But Aunt Enid, with whom the matter seemed to rest, was anxious above all things, not to appear to her sister and niece to have been defeated, or even adequately matched, in argument. This motive drove her forward into further argument. Thus when Mrs Lyte leaned forward on her chair as if in preparation to rise and move, her preparatory words misfired.

"Thank you very much, Father. It's been good of you to give us your time. We do appreciate what you have said—don't we, Elizabeth?"

"Of course."

"Speak for yourself, Margaret," Aunt Enid said tartly. "I'm not going to pretend that Canon Kirkbride's opinions have any effect on me."

The canon inclined his head in a gentle bow. It was done without any hint of patronage. The gesture seemed to say, You have the right to free speech: I have heard you: I shall not quarrel unnecessarily.

"Aunt Enid," said Elizabeth, blushing for her, "it isn't kind to say that. It's rude."

"Indeed," Mrs Lyte added quietly, "I think you owe the rector an apology, Enid."

"An apology!" Aunt Enid exploded. "You say that I should apologize to him, when I have had to listen to him vulgarizing the most sacred thing in the world."

"I have been accused of much in my time," the

canon said gently. "But not previously, I think, of vulgarity."

"Belief in God has a strange effect on some people," Aunt Enid continued. "It makes them drag fine human emotions through the mud."

"Miss Prynne," the canon said, becoming crisper all of a sudden, "if we are going to dispute, let's do it with some dignity and coolness."

"Who is not cool?" Aunt Enid asked, nearly boiling.

"Well, let's at least be lucid." The canon amended his first suggestion, perhaps having decided that it was too ambitious. "You do not believe in God?"

"Not in your God."

"Not in any God?"

"There is a living force in Nature. It is there all around us. It impels the flowers to grow and the birds to sing. It drives us to seek food and possessions and comfort. It makes us fall in love. If you call that God . . ."

"I don't," the canon said, "for I take it that you refer to some principle of growth in the natural order—but not to some power which stands outside and above the natural order."

"There is no such power," Aunt Enid said.

"Of course I don't sympathize with that point of view," the canon said, "but I understand it. It is clear, and very learned men have sometimes held it. It means that we must regard human beings as products of nature and nothing more; the crowning achievement hitherto of an evolutionary process. The process is there. It operates. But it has no meaning outside itself. No God devised it or set it going. It works to no end beyond itself. It is not dependent upon anything greater than itself."

Aunt Enid nodded. She was surprised at the clarity which the canon displayed in summing up views which he detested. There was a positive stirring of sympathy within her, as she heard her own philosophy expressed more concisely than she could have expressed it herself.

The canon put his finger to his lips and he creased his forehead. He seemed to be thinking hard.

"It means, I suppose, that all our human urges—our desire for success and comfort and well-being, and our appetites for food, possessions, and sex—all these are themselves products of the natural order. There is nothing higher than nature which can implant impulses and aspirations in man, so they must be the products of nature."

He spoke as though grappling with the problem. Aunt Enid assumed a less prickly, more helpful tone.

"They must be, as you say."

"It's an interesting theory." Canon Kirkbride sounded as though it were new to him and he were weighing its merits for the first time. "But it does leave one little difficulty. I can't quite see my way through it. Perhaps you can help."

Aunt Enid smiled. She was flattered. More important, she suddenly felt that she was needed. That there was something for which she, and she alone—not Margaret, nor Elizabeth—was required.

"You see," the canon went on, "you have said that love between the sexes is the most sacred thing in the world. You did make that point, didn't you?"

"I believe it is," Aunt Enid said firmly.

139

"You would argue that it is so sacred that we have no right to impose rules and regulations which limit it in any way?"

"No rule can be allowed to interfere with anything so spontaneous and sacred as a relationship of love between two free people."

"I see. Sexual love is so sacred that if it conflicts with the marriage vow, then the vow must be broken?"

Aunt Enid nodded. For one fleeting second she was on the brink of indulging the impossible thought that perhaps Canon Kirkbride was being converted from the superstitions of a life-time.

The canon removed his glasses and stared at the lenses.

"What gives sexual love its sacredness?"

Aunt Enid assumed a puzzled expression and did not reply.

"If sexual love is a mere product of natural evolution —like the appetite for food or the urge to possess things —what is there in it which gives it this sacred quality? Whence derives this mysterious, dramatic compulsiveness, which means that home, children, pledges of fidelity, and faithful partners themselves can all be properly sacrificed to it? What is the secret of this powerfully sacred aura investing sexual love?"

"It is self-evident," Aunt Enid said. "It requires no explanation."

"You see my difficulty. We Christians believe that sexual love can be given a sacred significance by God. We believe it can be sanctified by the Church and offered up to God in the sacrament of marriage. But this sacredness investing married love is derived from

God's blessing upon the marriage: and God's blessing is given only on the exchange by the two parties of life-long vows. Now whence does the sacredness of sex derive for you? If you have no God to bless the human and the earthly, no God to whom earthly or human things can be dedicated, how can anything within this natural order be more sacred or binding than anything else? How can the sexual urge be given a mystical authority if there is no divinity from whom a significance higher than that of the natural can be derived? And if the sexual urge has no mystical authority, why do so many non-Christians sacrifice their homes, their children, their spouses, and so much else to it?"

Aunt Enid did not reply. The argument was taking her a little out of her depth. The journals which fed her week by week with gibes at prelates in the gossip columns and highbrow pornography on the book pages —these journals were not exactly strong on the philosophical side, and did little to encourage their readers in logical thinking. She was well-equipped with an emotional feeling—the residuum of much cursory reading—that the Church was wicked and uninhibited sex was pure, but she couldn't rake up arguments or evidence. Indeed the harder she thought, the more she began to suspect that her trusted journals had not been so lavish in supplying arguments as they might have been.

"I will tell you the answer," the canon said, speaking with great deliberation. "The contemporary anti-Christian who believes that all we have and are has been produced by the chance evolution of the natural order has not been consistent. He has invested sex with a pseudo-religious significance, transcending the significance of marriage-vows, filial ties, parental obligations, and ordinary decent considerateness towards those who have served and been faithful. He has expunged religious significance from the universe, only to reintroduce it by the back door in the sphere of sex. From all else upon the human scene he has stripped off the sacred, the mystic, the compulsive—and then he has endowed sexual experience with all these qualities. It is illogical, irrational, incongruous: but it has been done.

"Sex is the God of the post-Christian West. Sex is worshipped as only divinities can properly be worshipped. Sex is obeyed as only the absolute commands of supernatural authority can properly be obeyed. Sex is exalted and glorified. Sex is meditated upon and contemplated. Sex is hymned and hailed and bowed down before. The idolatrous images of this unholy cult are before us on every street and in every paper. The garish temples of this cult dominate the centres of our greatest cities. From childhood upwards we train our future citizens in the full cultivation of this superstitious idolatry—train them by means of the press, the cinema, the television, the hoarding, the shop-window. Our civilization has decided that, whatever may be known or unknown of other gods, other idols, other cults, at least this one thing shall be certain: that every human being who grows to maturity in our midst shall, before he reaches adulthood, have his mind, his imagination, and his heart, soaked, stifled, sodden with sex."

This speech had a peculiar effect upon Aunt Enid, which was quite the reverse of what might have been expected. As long as the canon spoke coolly, with his crisp logic and tight arguments, he merely antagonized Aunt Enid all the more. But when, for a moment, he forgot himself, when he allowed himself to be carried away with emotional fervour through the very force of his conviction and the depth of his displeasure, then Aunt Enid's hostility and irritation melted away. Suddenly she saw in Canon Kirkbride something that existed so powerfully in herself—a burning, white-hot fervour which was too full of thrust and passion to be contained. She caught the reflection of an inner fire which could leap, shrivel, and consume. Here was an affinity all too rarely glimpsed. He too knew what it was to burn.

In a sudden fit of emotion, unaccountable to the canon, she dabbed one eye with a handkerchief.

"I'm not going to argue," she said awkwardly.

That was all. It left Mrs Lyte and Elizabeth equally in the dark. It plunged the canon into a teasing uncertainty. Then she rose, and the others rose too. Goodnights were said. And it was not long before the canon was on his knees.

7

"Sit down," said Canon Kirkbride. "I'm glad you've come. I hoped you would."

The canon was wearing his cassock. This, thought Howard, was a bit much. Even without that addition the study stank of the Church. In the far corner, opposite the window, there was a prayer desk and, behind it, a crucifix hung on the wall. The bookshelves bulged, not only with upstanding books, but also with horizontal volumes, papers, and folders. There were statues on the mantelpiece and a framed photograph on every available flat surface. The table at which the canon worked was laden with typewriter, open Bible, other books, and loose papers. It appeared that a sermon was in preparation. How keep one's head in a room so charged with atmosphere?

"You've got everything in here, Padre, except a harmonium."

The canon remained unsmiling. The habitual resort to flippancy was no doubt to be expected. It was in part the product of nervousness. But it was not to be encouraged here. The canon knew well the psychology of that contrived frivolity by which men like Howard Prentice preserve themselves from self-exposure. Frivolity of that kind could feed itself fat on the sparest diet of responsiveness. It had to be killed by slow starvation.

"I've come to talk to you about this difficulty I'm in."

"Difficulty?" The canon feigned a naïve surprise.

"My connection with this divorce case."

"Oh yes."

"You will have seen that it has got me into the papers. Damned bad luck, really."

"I have heard about the matter," Canon Kirkbride said pensively, as though he were already grappling with the problem.

"It has made a mess of things, hasn't it?"

"In what way?" the canon asked, somewhat to Howard's surprise.

"Well, it has put me in this difficult position with the Lytes. The old man is frightfully sore. And Elizabeth isn't even seeing me. Pretty difficult, you must admit. And all through some fool of a journalist."

Canon Kirkbride again looked like one who had lost the thread.

"These words *difficult* and *difficulty* are confusing. To what do they refer?"

"To this divorce case and my unfortunate connexion with it."

The canon rubbed his forehead with the palm of his hand.

"What is it that you find most trying in this matter?"

"The publicity."

"I see." The canon screwed up his eyes and pursed his lips. "If it were not for the publicity, you wouldn't mind so much."

"I shouldn't. That's what makes it such a thundering let-down. If only the thing could have been kept quiet!"

The canon shook his head gravely.

"I was wondering whether perhaps you had any personal regrets for your part in the story."

"Oh certainly."

"What do you find most regrettable?"

"The fact that Elizabeth has taken it so badly. I expected it of the old man. But Elizabeth! Well, I mean, it *is* the twentieth century, isn't it? Even you, Padre——"

"A moment, Mr Prentice. I'm beginning to follow you. When you described this matter of the divorce proceedings as a 'difficulty', you really meant that it was a difficulty—an obstacle?"

"That's right." Howard confirmed the obvious, wonderingly.

"An obstacle standing between you and the object of your desires?"

Howard nodded impatiently. The analysis seemed superfluous.

"And when you speak of regretting this obstacle, you mean that you would like to see it either surmounted or removed?"

"Exactly." Howard stared at the canon. Surely he had made all this quite clear.

But the canon looked at Howard only in quick intermittent glances. For the most part he stared at his own feet or into the fire.

"Suppose Elizabeth were the kind of girl—and the Lytes the kind of family—to whom a divorce was neither here nor there. Would you feel the same regrets?"

Howard could see now where this was leading. Canon Kirkbride was trying to pin some blame on him irrespective of Elizabeth's attitude: but he felt stubborn.

"If the divorce case were not an obstacle, the situation would be totally different."

"Or if your liaison were unpublished and unknown?"

"That would certainly have prevented any trouble."

Canon Kirkbride leaned forward in his chair.

"Perhaps you can see my own difficulty, Mr Prentice. By calling I am a priest. When people come to speak to me of their 'difficulties'—as they do from time to time—the word usually refers to circumstances against which they are struggling to sustain their own well-being and the well-being of their dependants; lack of money, ill-health, professional inadequacy, and that kind of thing. These indeed are difficulties, and one has to try to help people to cope with them and surmount them. But, as a priest, I receive people here whose unhappiness is of a different kind. They come to tell me of actions in their past lives which lie heavily on their consciences. They come to speak of their own shortcomings, their own sins. It is my duty to help them to penitence and, if they ask it, to give them formal absolution.

"Perhaps a man finds it a hard struggle to support his family and keep up with his Hire Purchase payments. That is his difficulty. He needs to be advised about it, and helped. Perhaps, in a moment of pressure,

147

he has obtained some money dishonestly. That is his sin. He needs to repent of it and to make restitution. You will see that I cannot give fruitful advice unless the line of demarcation is clearly drawn between difficulties and sins."

"I see the point." Howard could not dispute the logic, though the application of the argument to his own case threatened to be ruthlessly uncomfortable.

"You will expect me to be frank," Canon Kirkbride went on. "I cannot see your situation as fraught with difficulties that have to be surmounted. I can see sins that ought to be repented of."

"There are difficulties too. Even if we call my liaison a sin, it still stands in the way of my marrying Elizabeth."

The canon shook his head. He seemed unwilling to concede anything at all to Howard.

"If a man cannot support his family, that, in my eyes, is an unquestionable difficulty, because we are all agreed at the outset that it is a good thing that his family should be supported. It is God's will that his children should be fed. But not every obstacle that stands between a man and his desires is a difficulty of that kind. Far from it. It may be a good thing that you should marry Elizabeth. It may be God's will that you should. But we cannot be sure at the outset that it is so. Especially when Elizabeth herself is apparently unconvinced."

There was a rueful irony for Howard Prentice in the canon's theoretical elimination of his problems. It seemed like a deadlock before consultation had begun. It was like the deadlocks over procedure which paralyse international conferences before any issues have been raised. Since Canon Kirkbride was the last man to compromise, Howard decided that he would have to give ground himself.

"I'm not pretending to be blameless over this liaison. I admit that I was in error there."

"In error—do you really mean in error?"

"Well," Howard shrugged his shoulders. "I suppose I ought to have known better than to fall for a married woman."

"Known better—or done better?"

"I said known," Howard repeated, a little nettled now to have his statements probed as though he were a schoolboy translating Latin.

"Error is not always blameworthy. A man may be in error through no fault of his own. Error is false thinking and reasoning. Perhaps you thought it was right and proper to make love to another man's wife?"

"No, I didn't."

"Then you did *know* better?"

Howard sucked in his cheeks. The canon had caught him out.

"All right. You win. I did the wrong thing."

"Wrong?" the canon queried remorselessly. "Incorrect or evil?"

"Need we go in for this wholesale analysis of everything I say?"

"It may be the only way of getting at the truth. Our words may reveal or conceal the truth, from ourselves and from others. A man may acquire, by force of habit, a set of phrases that blur the moral quality of his actions and virtually destroy his moral judgment."

Howard Prentice felt that the canon could scarcely have accused him more openly of trying to disguise the facts. But he was weary of the long preamble, which prevented him from getting to grips with the subject of Elizabeth; so he bore it patiently and conceded the point.

"You want me to say that I did an evil thing, Padre."

"I want you to feel it."

For a few moments nothing was said. Canon Kirkbride stared gravely at the fire, his eyes strangely still before the flickering of the flames. Howard Prentice experimented imaginatively with the notion that making love to Mildred had been "evil". Would it help if he pictured her with horns sprouting out above and a tail behind? No. The canon was a dear, but it was quite absurd to try to make something black and demoniacal out of their trifling, amateurish game. They had scarcely scratched the surface of passion. Anybody who knew Mildred would have understood. Anybody who had seen her looking up at him, her head held in a conscious pose as though she were being photographed, the unfussy neatness of her black hair suggesting a fastidiousness quite foreign to her. Her Italian nose curved a little too harshly when her face was seen in profile, but it was a well-proportioned face, though her mouth, which curled upwards at the edges when she smiled, always looked as though it were well pleased with itself for being in the right place. When you looked at the mouth and chin only, you felt that she was perhaps self-satisfied; but her brown eyes changed all that. They had plaintiveness, if not depth.

Not that it was at all a voluptuous face. Hence perhaps her queer, unstable charm; for she often seemed to be trying to assume a voluptuous expression beyond the range of her static, tilted poses. That was her trouble; her unreality. She wasn't real to him, perhaps not to anyone, perhaps not to herself. Whereas Elizabeth was always real—not least when she refused to see him.

He took out a cigarette and steadied himself with three long pulls. Then he weighed in.

"Look here, Padre, I might as well be honest. I'm in love with Elizabeth. I'll do anything in my power to put myself right with her. I'm ready to admit I've been a swine in some ways. And I've certainly been a fool, or I shouldn't be in this absurd mess. If talking about my sins is going to put me right, then I'm ready to talk about them—on the radio, if you like. I'll go back to the year dot and make a list of the whole shoot. I could kick myself all right. You don't need to tell me what a bull's foot I've made. Oh, I know I don't use your phrases; but I think I mean the same thing as you."

"I wonder if you do. In all you say, you seem to be dominated by a single motive—that of gaining Elizabeth."

"I am."

"That isn't penitence. The penitent seeks nothing for himself—except forgiveness."

"Other things may follow."

"True. There may be other benefits. But frequently they turn out to be quite different from what we have expected. You see, as I have said before, it may be right that you should not marry Elizabeth. You ought to be prepared to face that."

Why did the canon harp on this so much? Howard felt there was something sinister in it. It couldn't be that the canon felt he ought to marry Mildred, for parsons didn't believe in remarriage. And anyway, quite apart from Elizabeth, that was utterly impossible now. The real decision about Mildred had been made four months ago, made in cold blood and then formally signalized at that rather squalid party when Nigel went to sleep, fully clothed, in the bath, and Roger remained obstinately half-drunk all night. How irritating Roger had been on that occasion! He patted Mildred's knees at she sat on the piano, with a paternal familiarity that was infuriating; enacting Howard's secession from her in public before he had had the chance to accomplish it privately. Roger was brilliant at these devastating symbolic acts that made his victims seethe. He had then lifted Mildred bodily from the piano and solemnly deposited her in Howard's lap; the gesture of a man patronizingly giving away something which he could very cheerfully dispense with—or restoring to its rightful owner a long-loaned and now somewhat damaged article.

Then that unsatisfactory scene when the break-up came; he trying to make a dignified last appearance, Mildred anticipating him on every point with a calculated burlesque of the statement he had privately rehearsed. He was an actor—it was her favourite gibe—an actor wanting a nice little tragic scene and going into a pet because his partner didn't play up. When he tried to be grave, she taunted him. "You want to leave me,

Howard, but you can't bear the thought of leaving me cheerful. You want to leave me in torment." Denials were useless. She was determined to be crude. She got what she wanted—a *post facto* devaluation of their whole relationship. From first to last it had been retrospectively vulgarized.

To turn from it all to Elizabeth was to walk out of a fog into the fresh air. Nothing was a stale game to her: there was no technique; no throwing of the ball between them: everything was new to her. And that was what made her so real and alive. There was no self-concealment. In everything she revealed herself, in acceptance and rejection alike. As when he first piled on the fervour in a dim corner of the Royal Lounge. It was astonishingly, incredibly electric. It was like the snatching of a virginity. Her lips quivered in accentuation of a nameless distress. "Howard, can't you see, can't you see? You talk of being in love; and the very words you use make it impossible for me to answer. I can't even listen." Then the gentle apology, the leaning forward, his hand on hers as she clasped them nervously, and the slight moistening of her eyes as she smiled at him her almost uncritical forgiveness.

Howard shook his head knowingly.

"We sit and talk about it here, Padre, as though the matter were in our hands. Yet the whole thing may already be quite settled elsewhere, and in my favour."

"How so?"

"Elizabeth may be in love with me still, right through. I have good reason to suspect that she is."

Canon Kirkbride looked him steadily in the eyes.

"How would that settle everything?"

"She'd *have* to marry me."

"Have to? Why 'have to'?"

"If she's really in love, she won't be able to help herself."

Canon Kirkbride sighed as though Howard's very obvious deduction constituted something remarkable.

"How little you understand us. It doesn't follow at all."

Howard began to lose patience.

"Look here, Padre, with all due respect, I'm ready to admit that you churchy people may have got something different. But you're not a different species. When a person falls in love, he's in love: and he can't do anything about that whether he's a Christian, a Buddhist, or a head-hunter. Being churchy can't put you above the laws of Nature."

Canon Kirkbride pounced eagerly.

"That's exactly what it does. It puts you above the laws of Nature. So that you can even be in love and say No."

Howard's folded thumb went to his lips as this point sank home, and his difficulties suddenly assumed a new magnitude. Elizabeth might even be deep in love and yet say No. If that were true, how could one have ordinary human relationships with people of this Kirkbride cult?

"I don't believe it. It would be a kind of treachery."

"Treachery to what?"

"To simple human honesty."

"I don't think so," the canon said. "There's nothing dishonest about saying, I'd like to have this, but I think it would be bad for me, so I won't. You make that kind of decision every time you look into a shop window."

"This isn't a question of possessions. It's a question of living human beings."

"True. Nature draws together two creatures, a man and a woman, with a violent mutual attraction. I'm afraid Nature is lawless in some ways. She doesn't pause to note that one of the parties is already married or betrothed—or perhaps has a duty to remain single. She ignores those refinements which we call morality and civilization. The world is her jungle. Christians are trained in resistance to Nature when she works like that. They have a code which instructs them to say No. They are in touch with a source of power which will enable them to say No. That is their treachery—to the order of Nature."

Howard grew more excited than ever.

"You are trying to tell me that Elizabeth . . ."

"Wait a moment," the canon said gently. "I am not trying to tell you anything about Elizabeth's intentions, feelings, or wishes over this particular matter. I am not authorized to do that. I am merely explaining to you the code which I know she and her parents accept."

"You are saying that, even if she were still violently in love with me . . ."

"She would not necessarily marry you for that reason alone; especially after impediments had been brought to her notice."

Howard frowned. The canon's confidence in speaking of Elizabeth was particularly significant.

"You have seen her very recently?"

"To-day."

155

"And she spoke to you about me?"

"A little."

Howard resented this. These people had a net around him. Ever since he had first met Canon Kirkbride, the issue between himself and Elizabeth had been confused by this confounded religion. It no longer seemed possible to get at her except through this labyrinthine ecclesiastical inquisition. Here he was, a full week after she had sent him the ring back, caught up in a web of dogmatic moralizing by a professional purveyor of taboos. "If there is anything not clear to you, see Canon Kirkbride." That had been Elizabeth's curt message. He had acted upon it, and it was getting him nowhere. He had not come here to-night for a sermon: nor had he come for a session of psycho-analysis. He had come for assistance, hoping to be able to clear up the formalities of getting himself right officially with Elizabeth—if not with her father. He had come in the hope of doing something about the future; and all Canon Kirkbride could do was to offer him his seamy past on a plate, telling him to eat it publicly and make himself sick with it. And all to no purpose apparently. For Elizabeth's decision was going to be made in accordance with some incomprehensible rules of conduct in an occult ecclesiastical text-book, drawn up to spread misery among human beings. He might just as well have stayed at home, or gone to the club. He would have got more encouragement from Roger.

Canon Kirkbride looked as though he were expecting Howard to speak.

"We seem to be back where we started from."

"With the original question of your liaison, and how you ought to feel about it."

"I can tell you that," Howard retorted hastily. "I'm sick of the whole business."

The canon nodded: but it did not look like satisfaction.

"As for the question of Elizabeth," Howard added. "It is not immediately relevant."

Howard turned impulsively on his tormentor.

"I won't be brow-beaten. It's relevant through and through. It's the mainspring of the whole problem. I'm not going to do anything at all, without . . . without . . ."

He fumbled for words. Canon Kirkbride found some.

"Without a guarantee that you'll get what you want out of it."

"Hell," said Howard, touched to the quick at last. "If I'm as bad as that, then I am. That's all."

The canon looked him squarely in the eyes.

"You're not," he said.

Howard didn't like the tone of piety. He pulled himself forward in his chair, as if preparing to rise.

"We're wasting each other's time."

"I hope not."

"We are."

"Well, it's more sociable than just wasting one's own time."

"We look at things differently," Howard said, in a patronizing tone, as though the very saying of it conferred a benediction. "We must agree to differ."

Canon Kirkbride frowned, took off his glasses, and

peered at them as though they carried some oracular secret inscribed in minute script.

"I don't think there is even that much agreement between us," he said.

"Oh," Howard smiled deprecatingly, preparing to make a tolerably courteous getaway. "It's not as bad as that, surely."

"Perhaps I'm not good at making myself clear. I've tried to make one point, only one. And I've failed, I think. I hoped you would pass judgment on your unfortunate liaison without any reference to your present hopes."

"I quite see that," Howard assured him. "I'm quite ready to admit that I made a howling blunder there."

Canon Kirkbride's jaw dropped ponderously.

"A blunder?" he queried.

"Looking back, I can see that. It was a pretty silly business all through."

The canon shook his head.

"Blunders are accidental miscalculations." He spoke deliberately. "I think there was something more than a blunder. As for being silly, I don't think that is your great weakness."

"You flatter me, Padre."

"Quite the reverse, if you did but understand. I judge you more harshly than you judge yourself."

"All right." Howard was irritated that the canon should have got back to this point again. It seemed to be an obsession with him. "You want me to use moral terms: to speak of black and white."

"Good and evil," the canon corrected him. "I hoped you might begin to think and feel in those categories."

"It hasn't been my habit."

"No. And that's why it's difficult for us even to agree to differ. We haven't a sufficiently common set of concepts between us."

"I'm sorry," Howard said, sensing a real distress in Canon Kirkbride, who obviously wanted to communicate with him only in his familiar professional phrases. "I must be honest. And, frankly, it doesn't come naturally to me to divide my past up into good bits and bad bits."

"It doesn't come naturally to anyone. That's what I've tried to say. It's a triumph over Nature to distinguish between good and evil."

"Like the triumph of being in love and saying No," Howard added sarcastically.

"Exactly."

"I think I like Nature's way best."

"We all do, in a sense. That's the kind of creatures we are. But we will ourselves to follow a different way."

"What way?"

"God's way."

"And how can we know what God's way is? And why should it differ from Nature's way?"

"Ah," said the canon, with a gleam of new zest in his eyes. "Those are big questions. They deserve big answers."

Howard waved his hand in impatient dismissal.

"Quite so," said the canon. "I'll put it briefly. And I'll take the second question first. Why should God's way differ from Nature's way? Because everything in human life that is good and worth-while depends upon restraining Nature—imposing a higher code upon her own lawlessness. Nature's way is the way of the animal —the play of appetite and desire unrestricted by consideration for the well-being of others. Human civilization is built upon the taming of man's appetites to possess, to dominate, and to indulge himself. To approve of civilization, as distinct from savagery, is to prefer the human way to Nature's way. God's way is higher than man's way, as man's way is higher than Nature's way.

"Man's way is to replace the jungle with the ploughed field and to replace the swamp with the city. God's way is to replace the lust of the eye and the greed of the heart with the joy of obedient filial service.

"And your second question. How do we know what God's way is? He has taken the trouble to show us. That is precisely the Church's message. He has taken the trouble to show us. Our Lord's way is God's way. The Church's way is our Lord's way. And the Church's way is penitence, faith, obedience."

Howard received this in silence, momentarily touched by the force of Canon Kirkbride's sincerity. So silent was he that Canon Kirkbride wondered whether he ought to go further. Studying Howard's tight lips and rapidly shifting eyes, he was inclined to think not. It was rarely a good idea, with unbelievers or half-believers, to answer questions that had not been asked. There were quite enough of the asked ones to answer. You cannot stampede the restless post-war sceptic into religion. And, although no doubt there are hungry minds all around us, it is ironically easy to overfill one. So the canon's next offer was a very tentative one.

"If you should want to go into these questions more fully at any time . . ."

Howard Prentice shook his head. He certainly did not want to be told again, in pedantic detail, exactly what the code was which could enable an otherwise honest girl like Elizabeth to be in love and at the same time to pretend that she wasn't. For that was what it seemed to amount to, whatever fancy name the canon gave to it. A code of organized hypocrisy; a blasphemous blessing upon the betrayal of one's deepest feelings.

"No, I think we've had enough tonight."

"As you wish."

Howard rose and turned towards the door.

"One moment," the canon said, going over to his desk. "I promised that, if you came to have a talk, I would give you this note. It's from Elizabeth."

Howard's foot tapped the carpet in restless irritation. So there had been collusion to that extent! A neat little conspiracy to finish him off finally without giving him the chance to explain. That was it, no doubt. He grasped the letter and thrust it into his pocket. Then he changed his mind, took it out, and opened it there and then.

Dear Howard,

I'm sorry if anything Daddy or I have done or said has seemed like rudeness. Being suddenly distressed made it difficult for us to act thoughtfully straight away. Now I am quite sure that I have reached the right decision.

I don't know what Father Kirkbride has said to you, but he's right, you know.   E.

Howard held the note open before the canon in a mood of intense disgust.

"God in heaven, how can an adult human being say that?—I don't know what he has said, but he's right. It's mental abdication."

"There's such a thing as trust," the canon said gently.

"Trust, yes. But to give a blank cheque of agreement to statements not yet thought of! You might have told me to go and poison my grandmother."

Canon Kirkbride raised his hands, and then dropped them helplessly to his sides.

"You cast a slur upon the deepest of all emotions; and then you bind yourself together in a kind of mystical agreement that defies common sense."

"There's some truth in that," the canon said quietly.

Howard crumpled up the letter and stuffed it into his pocket. He felt so deeply injured that he wanted to make some damaging retort.

"If this is what your God does to you, I don't want him."

The canon lowered his head and, for a moment, Howard felt ashamed of his outburst.

"In a sense none of us wants him. But he wants us."

Howard smiled ironically.

"He has a funny way of showing it."

"Yes; very often."

"And I don't think I can even agree to differ with him."

"That," said the canon, "is beyond your power to decide."

8

ROLAND WOULD never have dreamed in his wildest moment of getting Canon Kirkbride and Jago Bingley together in the same room. Indeed, if he had been asked to name two extreme incompatibles among his friends and acquaintances, he might well have chosen these two. Yet here they were, face to face, and he, as host, had somehow to conduct proceedings as though the most outrageous social incongruity were not after all being committed among them.

Jago Bingley, one of Roland's colleagues on the staff of Delphwick Grammar School, was here because Roland had invited him. And Roland had done so because, among a thousand dissimilarities, they shared an important common interest—the gramophone. Each had a small library of records which was something of a hobby. Roland collected chamber music and also some vocal work—chiefly sixteenth- and seventeenth-century polyphonic stuff. Jago Bingley collected orchestral works of the nineteenth century especially—the kind of thing which forms the backbone of popular programmes at symphony concerts. It was not uncommon for the two of them to meet, either at Jago's home or at Roland's, in order to show off recent acquisitions.

It was a peculiar relationship. They didn't really

agree about music at all. Secretly Roland felt that European music took the wrong turn somewhere around the first performance of the Eroica symphony ("when the explosion ousted the phrase," he used to say), whereas Jago was sure that European music came to maturity exactly at that same point. Roland liked the Haydn quartets and Palestrina: Jago went so far as to praise the César Franck and Elgar symphonies. In short there was every reason for them to argue, and they did. But there was little possibility that the two of them would ever buy the same record; and they didn't. The only two occasions on which the musical views of the two of them had seemed momentarily to coincide were, once, when Jago had protested that his orchestral enthusiasms did not reach out to embrace *Ein Heldenleben* and *Till Eulenspiegel* and, again, when Roland, in a yielding moment, had confessed to a weakness for Berlioz.

The somewhat competitive nature of their relationship as connoisseurs in rival schools of music expressed itself in frequent half-serious argument. There was between them an established habit of wrangling, not overtly, but obliquely. Each had cultivated a technique of depreciating the musical taste of the other by an indirect attack which was unsparing and yet not ill-humoured. When Jago demonstrated the last movement of Dvořák's G major symphony, Roland raised his eyebrows quizzically. "There are fellows, I know, who believe that this sort of thing will come back and be respectable again. You may be right in the swim in another ten years' time." And when Roland played his latest record from Schütz's Passion music, Jago screwed up his face into an expression of intense bewilderment. "You really *do* like to listen to this, don't you? I mean, you enjoy it musically? Not just as a matter of historical interest and all that. You really take pleasure in it?"

It was not difficult for Jago Bingley to assume the rôle of the totally uncomprehending, at sea in an alien environment. Physically he had the appearance of a man unconvinced. He was a wiry little man and something like a perpetual scowl creased his features. Moreover he kept his head permanently tilted to the right at an angle of forty-five degrees. This gave the impression of a personality involved in an interminable interrogation. He was ten years older than Roland, much his senior on the school staff, and felt justified in employing his heaviest irony at the expense of Roland's allegedly superior taste. He taught Latin, and had refined and perfected a slick, examination-winning system which was secretly the envy of his colleagues. His private system of working out in advance which passages from Virgil would turn up in G.C.E. was infallible. "It's only a question of collecting the data," he would explain. And the data consisted of a table of all extractable passages of various lengths in the *Aeneid* as a whole, along with examination papers for the last ten years, and various other highly technical clues of the kind which Classics masters can discuss with their peers.

Thus Jago Bingley had plenty of reasons for being a confident man. And there were plenty of musical grounds also for the existence of a faintly antagonistic atmosphere in Roland's drawing room that evening. All this, no doubt, helps to explain why, when Canon

Kirkbride joined them in conversation, points were worried at and tussled with which, on another occasion, might have been quietly allowed to pass.

Of course, that the canon should be there at all was unusual. He had called to see Mrs Tay, Roland's mother, who had recently come home from hospital after a serious internal operation. The canon's arrival had, from the start, broken up the musical evening, for Roland had taken him upstairs and lingered awhile. By the time the canon came downstairs again, Jago had cleared the records away, Roland had fetched in some cheese and biscuits and had opened a bottle of Cyprus wine. The canon was only too happy to accept the proffered hospitality.

It was the Cyprus wine which started things going. Jago, who was an out-and-out Tory, said something disrespectful about archbishops who interfere in politics. This shaft was not directed at the canon but at Roland who, as a rebel and a left-winger, had his own provocative views on the Cyprus problem. There was only one word more likely than the word "Cyprus" to set Jago and Roland at each other's throats, and that was the word "Suez". During the brief altercation about Makarios, Canon Kirkbride sensed that more violent antagonisms were likely to be aired if the conversation were not given a twist in another direction, and he endeavoured to change its drift. Eventually he was successful.

"Religion has always bedevilled politics," Jago said. "The proper thing is to separate the two completely. It's logical too. Religion has strictly no connection with politics."

Roland turned to Canon Kirkbride, seeking an ally. "Can you let that pass, Canon Kirkbride?"

The canon had no desire to be brought in as a political ally. He had his political opinions: but he did not judge this the occasion for airing them. He was the parish priest, on duty in his parish, and graver things might appropriately be touched upon.

"I think it's a pity to over-use these abstract nouns *religion* and *politics*. If you ask me about the relationship between religion and politics, I find it difficult to give a precise answer. It is just the same if you ask me what is the connexion between faith and economics, or between penitence and the exchange rate. Let us make the question concrete, and we can be precise in our answer. Let us ask: Is God concerned in any way with what the Prime Minister does about this issue or that? The answer is, Yes, certainly. God is concerned that every human judgment should be true, and that every human decision should be made in the interests of justice and charity."

Roland jumped in.

"That is as good as saying that religion and politics are closely intertwined."

"It is not," the canon said firmly. "Religion is the sphere of thought and action in which men give their attention directly to God. Politics is the sphere of thought and action in which men give their attention to the ordering and government of society. These are very different spheres of operation. Of course you may say that because God is concerned with both of them, therefore the two are closely related; but that is a poor way to use words. On that basis one could assert a close

167

relationship between ceramics and football pools on the grounds that men interest themselves in both as hobbies.

"By means of the word *religion* we have defined and delimited a certain sphere of activity; by means of the word *politics* we have defined and delimited another and very different sphere of activity. The progress of human understanding and achievement depends upon isolating and clarifying concepts and terms of this kind. To confuse and blur the boundaries of terms is to disseminate darkness. To sharpen them is to shed light. I'm afraid therefore that when a man says—as I have heard it said—'Politics is only applied religion', he is talking nonsense, and assisting towards the stripping from man of dearly-bought understanding. I have always noticed, by the way, that the people most prone to talk of politics or social affairs as the spheres of truly religious activity have usually been those most ready to dilute the quality of the essentially religious in its own proper sphere. No, let us keep our words distinct. We are going to need them badly."

Jago frowned and pushed out his lower lip in a mood of surprised agreement.

"That's right. There are things which are of public significance, and there are things which are only of private concern. How a nation is governed and how its economy is manipulated—that sort of thing concerns every citizen in his capacity as a voter and a wage-earner. But what a man believes is a private matter. We've got to have tolerance of course, but religion is for home consumption."

The canon shook his head in profound disagreement.

"No, no. That is not at all what I have said. Religion can never be private in that sense. If my religion teaches me that the rich ought not to exploit the poor, nor the strong to attack the weak . . ."

"As at Suez," Roland quietly interposed. But the canon ignored it.

"Then my religion impels me to a certain course of action in public affairs. Indeed my religion provides me with my code of action in these matters, as in all other matters, whether I am a Prime Minister, an M.P., or a mere voter."

"You're contradicting yourself," said Jago, crunching the words out of the side of his mouth, as he did when slightly irritated. "Now you're saying that religion does affect politics."

"I am saying," the canon went on, quietly and deliberately, "that my faith gives me my impetus and my direction in whatever sphere I choose to act."

"Then you're saying that religion enters into everything you do."

The canon put his hand to his brow.

"No. I am saying that God enters into everything I do. Religion is the sphere of activity in which I contact him directly in worship and prayer. That is what the word 'religion' means. Through the medium of this specifically religious life I seek a fellowship with God which I can carry with me into secular activity. I seek God's entry into my own life so that he will govern my thought and behaviour wherever I go and whatever I undertake. God's sphere is the whole of human activity, and indeed the whole of creation. The sphere of religion is the sphere of certain specific activities."

"Oh, well," said Bingley, "if you're going to bring God into it . . ." He shrugged his shoulders.

"How can I leave him out if we are talking about religion—or indeed about anything which he has made and which he directs?"

"I don't believe in him," Bingley said.

"You mean that you don't put your trust in him?"

"No. I mean that he doesn't exist. There is no God. No good and loving God, that is. For all I know, there may be a malignant one. Things often suggest that there is."

"What has driven you to that conclusion?"

"Experience," Jago said, grinding the word out between his teeth. His voice was naturally harsh and his articulatory system always seemed to operate like a mincing machine. Jago expected the canon to show some signs of being shocked; but he merely nodded his head and took out his pipe as though he were quite accustomed to hearing God's existence denied.

"Saddening experience it must have been," he said quietly.

Jago's thoughts leaped back some fifteen years.

"I once saw a naked baby impaled on the end of an Arab spear. If there were a good God, that kind of thing just could not happen."

The canon received this in silence.

"The problem of suffering," Roland said.

"I wonder if it is," the canon said.

There was no reply.

"Perhaps you could tell us yourself," the canon went on, turning to Jago.

"Tell you what?"

170

"Exactly what it was about the dead baby which makes you so sure that there is no good God. Not the fact of death surely, for you were aware before that day that all men must die."

"The suffering," Jago said.

"Whose suffering?"

"The baby's, of course."

The canon eyed his pipe gravely, halting in the process of filling it with tobacco.

"I don't want to sound heartless. I agree that the spectacle you describe is a horrible and saddening one. But there might not have been much actual suffering. Perhaps a single blow and then blackness. Let us suppose that happened. The baby was knocked unconscious, stabbed to death, and then stuck on the spear. In fact the total experience of pain in that child's life must have been comparatively slight, less by a good deal than he might have experienced had he lived through the teething stage, far less than he would have experienced had he lived a long life and died a 'natural' death from cancer of the lung. Yet we are more shocked by that child's death than by the lingering, painful death of a man of seventy."

"What does that prove?" Jago asked.

"That pain itself is not the real problem—theoretically speaking."

"Ah," said Jago. "But it wasn't only the baby itself that suffered. It was someone's child. Presumably it had a mother."

"True. Was that much in your mind at the time?"

"No," Jago admitted, a little reluctantly. "To be honest, I don't think it was."

"And would your horror and disgust have been any the less if you had been told that the baby was an orphan without a friend in the world?"

Slowly Jago shook his head.

"The thing was horrible enough without respect to possible parents."

"Or to the precise degree of pain experienced?"

"Yes."

There was a moment's quiet. Then Roland intervened.

"I can't see where this argument is leading us."

"To this conclusion," the canon said. "That what we call the problem of pain is certainly always a problem, but it is not always about pain."

"Whatever it is," Jago said, "it stirs you to disgust with the world we live in."

"Exactly. That's what I'm getting at. Whether the baby felt pain or not, the spectacle you say aroused passionate disapproval. 'It oughtn't to be allowed.' That is the appropriate human response to spectacles like that. Suppose a girl is drugged and strangled. Suppose she feels no pain at all. And suppose she has no family and no devoted friends who suffer in losing her. Are we any the less shocked because the whole crime is accomplished without any person suffering? Suffering or no suffering, we still say, 'It oughtn't to be allowed.' It is not in essence the problem of human pain. It is the problem of human disapproval."

Jago nodded his head in ferocious agreement.

"But of course. That's what I'm saying. These things arouse anger in us. You call it human disapproval. Well and good. And what is it we disapprove of? It is disapproval of the kind of life into which we have been born. It is disapproval of whatever purpose it is that works through our long human story of unhappiness and disease and death. We disapprove. We say it isn't good. I agree with you. It certainly isn't good. And what does that mean? It means that there can't be a good God operating this system. It means that, if there is a God at all, then he must be a cruel one."

The canon at last finished packing his pipe, and he applied the first match to it. He got it going just in time to let it out during his reply.

"Wait a moment, Mr Bingley. This is a little too wholesale. We have had two examples. The impaling of a baby on a spear, and the strangling of a girl. But neither of these tragedies was due to what you might call a natural accident—like the eruption of a volcano; nor even to an unnatural accident, like a train crash. In each case the cruelty was consciously inflicted: the evil action was conceived and executed by a human being. How is God to blame for that?"

"If there is a God, then presumably he made human beings. He is responsible for the kind of creatures they are."

" Responsible for the fact that they are free creatures: not for the fact that they abuse their freedom. You can be responsible for sending your son to the university. You can't be morally responsible if he robs a bank while away from home."

During the pause which followed this point, Roland took the opportunity to hand round the biscuits again and fill up the wine-glasses.

"I badly need another drink myself," he said. "I'm

in rather a whirl. I can usually see where your argument is going, Father; what you're driving at, I mean. Usually I can catch a glimpse of the destination in the distance. It's quite good fun watching you get there; often by what seems at the time to be a circuitous route. But this time I'm in a fog. You've got me baffled. I'm not even sure whether you two are agreeing furiously, or quarrelling gently. It might be either."

"I never quarrel gently," Jago said.

"And I rarely agree at all passionately," the canon added with a smile.

Roland sat down again, and took a cigarette from a box on the mantelpiece.

"Seriously, where have we got to?"

The canon pressed his finger tips together with outstretched hands. It was a reposeful, recollective gesture.

"We haven't got anywhere yet. We're still *en route*. But there's a stopping-place in sight now."

"I can't see it," Jago said.

"Look," the canon said, directing his attention at Jago. "Would you admit that tragedies of the kind we have referred to arouse a double disapproval in many decent human beings—first, disapproval of the evil and cruel acts; a disapproval directed at the perpetrators: and secondly, disapproval of the total system or situation in which things like that can take place?"

"Agreed," Jago said. "And the second kind of disapproval is directed against what you call God."

The canon raised his hand.

"One step at a time. I want to analyse these disapprovals further. The first says, 'This is a wicked act committed by a wicked man.' That is moral judgment

174

or censure. The second says, 'This kind of thing ought not to be possible.' That is rebellion against the human situation."

"Surely," said Roland, breaking in, "that's exactly what Jago himself said."

"Let us examine the nature of this rebellion," the canon went on. "The only way by which wicked men could be prevented from doing wicked deeds of this kind would be by some restraint upon their freedom. To rebel against the situation which allows wicked men to practise their wickedness is to rebel momentarily against the full range of human freedom. But it is human freedom which makes your rebellion possible. Because you are free, therefore you can protest against the state of affairs in which freedom is granted. That is the extreme and maximum exploitation of freedom— the use of freedom to criticize freedom. But can a man logically criticize freedom when, in doing so, he is exploiting his freedom to the maximum? It does not make sense. It is a contradiction; an absurdity. For man to rebel against human freedom is a kind of lunatic self-contradiction. It is like making a long speech in criticism of the gift of utterance to human beings."

Jago ran his fingers through his already untidy hair as though he were at a loss to know how to drive home the point which the canon so signally failed to understand.

"Your argument is no argument," he said. "It doesn't reply to my case. No. It intensifies my case. I say the world is a miserable, unhappy world. I say there's no good God at the back of it, for if there were, we shouldn't have to look at so much cruelty and injustice. Very well. Then you tell me that freedom produces our ills, and that it's self-contradictory to rebel against freedom. You're merely underlining how hopeless our lot is. If we're in that kind of world—where we can't even logically say how bad it is without cutting the ground from under our own feet—then it's a cruel world indeed. That's what I said to begin with. All you are doing is to make it sound even worse.

"If there were a good God who had created a good universe, then what you say would be as unthinkable as what I say. We're both grumbling at life's rottenness. Only I'm doing it rebelliously and you're doing it apologetically."

The canon took a very deep, slow breath, staring directly ahead of him at the wall above Jago's head. This was a formidable argument. Of course there were good answers. But something more than mere reasoning was needed to touch a man like Bigley, who was probably clever enough to take any statement and involve it in his circular condemnation of life as a whole.

Roland began to wonder why Canon Kirkbride did not make use of his full dialectical powers at this point.

"When I said something like that to Canon Kirkbride," he said, "he dealt with my argument pretty neatly, I thought. I said the world looked to me like a rotten world and the human lot a meaningless one. Father Kirkbride then proved that my judgment on this life in this world was evidence that I was not fundamentally adapted to it or equipped for it—but for another life in another world. Somehow he made me convinced that we can only pass judgment upon this life by virtue of our inner attachment to another, superior order of things. It is in the light of our attachment to that superior order that we distinguish here between good and evil, right and wrong. I think that's a pretty watertight case."

Canon Kirkbride thought, but he did not say, that this argument had knocked Roland over for the very good reason that he was already, at the time when he encountered it, in the appropriate mental and emotional state to receive it and embrace it. He was fresh from an encounter with pain and death which had stirred to the depths his sense of the mysterious and the beyond, and left him acutely sensitive to the fact that life on earth cannot be understood as an end in itself. It was not possible to manufacture the full sense of the mystery of things in a comfortable suburban drawing room over wine and biscuits. Argument could go but a little way towards hinting at it.

"Speaking in terms of pure reason," he said, "and without reference to revelation, I think it is true that we have to be prepared, at some point in our argument about the meaning and value of life, to posit a possible life beyond this life. Certainly it would be highly irrational to rule it out as a possibility in advance of collecting and considering the evidence. As long as a life beyond this life remains to the mind as even a possibility, so long the mind must necessarily allow also for the possibility of realizations in that life beyond which will cast an entirely new light on experience here. Especially on the particular kind of experience which at present seems purposely harsh and tortuous. Reason will not allow us to dispense with these possibilities. Their survival as possibilities is the logical minimum that will satisfy reason. Do you agree?"

"Yes." Bingley dragged the word out laboriously. "I think I can allow that."

"Good." The canon's tone became more confident. "If we so much as allow for the possibility of future understanding which will transform our view of painful human experience, then we cannot argue from that experience to a decisive condemnation of life as a whole."

Which is what Jago was doing, Roland thought; but he was too tactful to say so.

Jago himself merely uttered a long, thoughtful "Hmmmmm" which seemed to say, There's an awful lot in that which needs to be thought about.

"I once came across a parishioner whose attitude might interest you," the canon said. "It was not in this parish, by the way. He was called Heap. He worked in a bank, and liked it. He was keen and had been several times promoted. Just after I left the district I heard that he had become the manager of a branch. I mention this to show you that he was an intelligent, active-minded fellow in his own way. He led a very ordinary, suburban, semi-detached existence with his wife and one child, a boy of six when I first met the family. Heap had no religion and was quite impervious to any spiritual challenge or appeal. It was not that he resisted the religious view; but he never seemed seriously to entertain it for a moment. I don't think any notion of spiritual things had ever penetrated into his mind.

"He was obsessed with an extraordinary idea. He thought birth a disgusting and cruel process utterly

178

unjustifiable. He had seen his own son born. 'Never again,' he would say, shaking his head knowingly. 'Oh no. It's quite wrong, quite wrong that any woman should have to go through that. Once you've seen it, that's enough for a life-time. No wife of mine will ever give birth again.'

"I used to try to argue with Heap, but it was no good. He lacked the speculative capacity to relate this view to other propositions which might corroborate or refute it. It was an isolated conviction built upon a single concrete experience. However, let's get at the main point. It's this. I've met thousands of parents in my time, and talked to them about their families. And I've never met one who expressed the same view as Heap. Indeed, whenever I've quoted Heap's view to other parents, invariably they have laughed at it. I would seem to be justified in concluding that parents in general find that view not only absurd, but rather comically absurd. Why do they find it so?"

"Presumably," Jago said, "because they think life is worth living and children are worth having, and a bit of discomfort at birth is negligible by comparison."

The canon nodded.

" 'A bit of discomfort' is a man's phrase," he said, "but there are no women here, so we'll let it pass. Heap's view was ridiculous. He concentrated on one aspect of a great and rich total experience, and by so doing he developed a perverted and infinitesimally narrow view of it which was quite laughably lop-sided."

"You're not going to associate my view with that. . ." Jago began.

"Well, not exactly," the canon said, hesitantly. "I mean, I'm not trying to suggest that you and Heap would have got on together like a house on fire."

"Thank you," Jago said heavily.

"There's an analogy here," the canon said, "that's all. You see, time after time, in the fifteen years since I met that man Heap, his view has come back to my mind in a peculiar way. Whenever I have been faced with some spectacle of almost unendurable grief or pain and I've said inwardly, 'Oh, God, you can't allow this, you can't!' then my thoughts have gone back to Mr Heap, sitting there at his fireside and shaking his head knowingly. 'Oh no. Never again. Not for Herbert Heap.' The question I ask myself is this. When we protest about earthly pain and misery, do we, in God's ears, sound like Mr Heap? Is that what our protest looks like in the sight of God who sees, not only this life, but the greater life to which it is subordinate? Are we all Mr Heaps? All of us—or most of us? Cut off from the big view, and magnifying a limited and inadequate view into an absurdly lop-sided attitude?"

The canon paused a moment and when he took up his case again, it was in a quiet and almost awesome voice.

"You may think this, that I am going to say now, is a shocking thing for anyone to say or think. Sometimes I think myself that it is. Yet the force of logic drives me to it.

"Mr Heap's protest against birth provoked laughter —and from sensitive, balanced men and women. Laughter. Think what that means. For, after all, in its essence, Mr Heap's protest was against a degree of

180

pain which no man has the right to belittle and which doctors tell us we are scarcely likely to exaggerate. Then how can it be that the protest against this pain can be transmuted into a cause of smiles in charitable men—and even in women who know that pain themselves?

"If this transmutation is possible, dare we perhaps try to conceive a state of mind and of spiritual poise—beyond this world, of course—in which our human protest against the very harshest of human pains and griefs has been so transmuted, so involved in a wider vision, that it can be held in the light grasp of an indulgent smile? An understanding smile, of course, and a sympathetic one. But still, a smile.

"I don't know. I don't know. But if it's right for healthy-minded men and women to smile indulgently at Mr Heap's disproportionate protest against the pain of labour, then perhaps God smiles affectionately upon every human protest against suffering. Not because he underestimates the suffering; but because, in the scope of his unlimited understanding, it looks so different. Not good in itself, of course. But by comparison with what eternally is, so infinitesimally small—and so indisputably worth-while."

There was quietness for a few moments after this: then slowly, gravely, Jago began to shake his head.

"I cannot conceive of any state of existence from which human misery could look less or other than it is. Or perhaps I can," Jago corrected himself thoughtfully. "Yes, granted that heaven were a state of topsy-turvydom presided over by a madman, then I suppose those inhabiting the place could laugh their heads off at war and disease and child-murder . . ."

"Be fair," Roland said. "Canon Kirkbride didn't say anything like that."

"I know he didn't. But his case seems to me to lead to that if you follow it to its logical conclusion. A lunatic heaven in which the surest and justest disapprovals of earthly life become matter for jest. The trouble with that theory is that it fits all the facts. On a strictly rational basis you could make a good case. A mad God is better than a bad God any day. After all a bad God is a contradiction in terms, but a mad God is just absurdity elevated to the nth degree. And life *is* absurd. There's no doubt about that."

Canon Kirkbride said nothing. He wondered. Perhaps he had said too much already. The line he had chosen seemed to have stirred up a fruitless sequence of thoughts in Jago. But then, abruptly, in the silence, Jago's ironical mood dropped from him. He leaned forward and there was a new earnestness in his voice.

"Canon Kirkbride, you have told me the story of Mr Heap to make your point. I'll tell you another story, which will make my point. It's a true story. My father told it many times. It concerned his closest friend —in their early days. This friend was a young man called Clive Howarth. My father was born and brought up in Reading. He got to know Clive when the two of them were about eighteen years old. My father became a regular visitor at their house. The Howarths lived next door to a family called Wadham. Mrs Wadham was a widow and she had two daughters, Miriam and

Heather. They were eighteen and sixteen years old when the awful thing happened.

"Well now, the Howarths and the Wadhams were both very good church-going families. They were not just ordinary attenders, you know, but the kind who got up early in the morning during the week and go to church before breakfast. Clive Howarth was brought up like that and so were the Wadham girls next door. The two families were mixed up with each other for everything—virtually a single family, my father used to say. Now my father had not had any religion in his upbringing at all. And he was very impressed by the devout ways of these two families and the generosity and happiness that seemed to spring from their religion. Clive began to take him to church and talk to him about his beliefs. For Clive was very earnest and always said that, if he could get hold of the money to educate himself, he would like to be ordained. It wasn't so easy then, before the First World War, for ordinary people to go in for things like that. Well, Clive was a great friend to my Dad; and my Dad thought he was the best fellow in the world. And he was sure Clive and Miriam would get married eventually.

"Then it happened. Suddenly. Like a bombshell. It was December 1912. Mrs Wadham took the girls up to London to do some Christmas shopping. They went into a store. The girls were very interested in some things in the basement, and Mrs Wadham wanted to visit some other departments upstairs. So she left them for a time, saying she'd come back and collect them there. She hadn't been gone long when a woman in nurse's uniform came along to the girls and said, 'I'm sorry. Your mother has had a slight accident. Nothing very serious. I'll take you to her. Come this way.' A shop assistant overheard this conversation. The girls followed the 'nurse' out of the department. That was all." Jago paused and lifted both hands in a gesture of hopelessness. "Nothing has been heard or seen of them since that day."

Canon Kirkbride closed his eyes. Roland's mouth fell open.

"The mother had a breakdown shortly afterwards," Jago went on quietly. "But, with the war, my father lost touch with both families. Clive was killed in action in 1914. It was the end of a lot of things, that December afternoon in 1912. It was the end of religion for my father. That and the war. He never forgot how God looked after those two devoted girls of his, so that they finished up in a brothel in Buenos Aires—or wherever it was."

The silence was deathly. All three sat listening to the faint hum of the electric fire.

"To think," Jago added bitterly. "They may be still alive. Miriam sixty-three and Heather sixty-one. What would they look like—with forty-odd years of it behind them; forty-odd years of . . ."

"Don't," the canon interrupted quietly.

"It's as bad as anything I've heard," Roland said. "I suppose the white slave traffic was pretty lively in those days. They've cleaned it up now, haven't they?"

No one answered.

"Of course," Jago went on. "I can't pretend that I feel this thing as my father used to feel it. What it had meant to him, you could tell by the way he told the

184

story. He knew the girls. They'd become a part of his life, week by week. But anyone with a bit of imagination can get a glimmering of what that poor widow went through—and Clive, and everyone else near to the girls. I've seen a photograph of the two of them, taken during the summer before they disappeared. Just the girls in the garden with the house behind. Cheerful, trusting kind of faces—and both frightfully beautiful. They paid heavily for that."

The canon remained silent. Jago's harsh, crunching voice had acquired an excited ironical squeak that was almost hysterical. The quiet after it was like the quiet that follows the clanging of a bell or the scream of a siren. You could hear it.

"It's the contrast." Jago's voice was harsher, squeakier still. "The photograph. Two girls with so much happiness before them. Then all the squalid painting and posturing of prostitution. So much freshness. Then so much putridity."

"No, no," the canon said. "This isn't right. We don't know what happened to the girls, or how they lived—or died. We don't know. We must judge what we do know. That's bad enough without additional inventions."

"It must have been white slave merchants," Roland said.

"I don't doubt that for a moment," the canon said. "It must have been."

"Then we can assume they finished up in a brothel." Jago almost snarled. "And I reckon we can posit syphilis too."

The canon fixed him with his eyes.

"The worst you could imagine for them would be that they became prostitutes and rotted themselves away, body and soul, with twenty years of drink and sex and another twenty of pimping. Put it in its crudest form, if you're so minded. It's a pure hypothesis anyway. And what about the other extreme? Now we've had the worst, what's the best you could imagine for them?"

Jago was silent. Roland tried to cooperate.

"That they somehow managed to escape," he suggested.

"Or perhaps," the canon said gravely, "that they refused and were dealt with—martyred for their faith. That too is a pure hypothesis. As such, it carries a certain weight, as does Jago's hypothesis. Between these two extremes lies a whole range of other possibilities, with their varied and enormous openings for both squalor and sanctity." The canon shook his head solemnly. "There is enough known sin and suffering in that story. Let us not be too ready to manufacture more."

Jago smiled grimly.

"I don't think there's much need to manufacture facts. A little bit of common sense is enough to give you an idea of what probably happened. With the best will in the world a girl hasn't much chance in that line these days. You don't need to charm her with new hats and dresses or to force her crudely. The hypodermic will deal with the most difficult.

"No. It's out-of-date to talk of girls refusing. The old-fashioned idea of the chaste woman resisting to the death was very touching and romantic, but it doesn't fit the facts of the twentieth century. Drugs have changed all that. Pump in the right injections and you can have a whole convent of nuns screaming for coition."

Canon Kirkbride was not squeamish, but his hand went up in protest against this example. Jago, feeling that he might be able to stampede the canon simply by being outrageous, tried to shock him further.

"You parsons are out of touch, you know. Have you never heard of marijuana or hemp? Why, there's no limit to what an ordinary decent girl will do when she's had all the pride and the shame smoked out of her. I've seen it—and not very far away. Not prostitutes either, but ordinary girls on a night out; moving about in a dream, with misty eyes, and ready to behave like animals. Well, when you've seen what can be done with one of those weeds that this God of yours has so thoughtfully scattered about the earth, then you can have a pretty good idea of what happened to those two Wadham girls. And when you think, by contrast, of their home and their upbringing and their mother, and what their lives were going to be, then it's enough to cure you of religion."

The canon realized that an enormous and confused growth of emotion and prejudice was entangled with Jago's rejection of religion. These moving stories—of the Arab spear and the Reading girls—were not the cause of his rebellion, but symbols of it. This was apparent in the fact that Jago seemed to relish, rather than regret, the inferences he drew from these tragic instances. Indeed the canon had observed life long enough to know that true tragedy rarely turns people from God. The direct experience of tragedy is more likely to fling men at God's feet. But the spectacle of tragedy, encountered at second hand, is readily exploited as additional evidence by those who have already decided that there is no good God.

The most the canon felt he could do was to weaken the melodramatic flavour given to this story, which befuddled reasoning.

"It's a shocking story, Mr Bingley. There's no doubt of that. But however beastly the criminals were, and however virtuous or religious their victims were, you still cannot blame God for what happened, unless you are prepared to protest against the freedom he has given us. We have to accept that this is precisely what God's gift of freewill to man involves—man's ability to steal and sell the virginity of another man's daughters. Intellectually we have to accept it."

"That sounds pretty callous to me," said Jago.

"Callous? Why?"

"To take the suffering of those girls in that cold way, as though it were a mathematical problem."

"Wait a moment," the canon broke in again. "We must distinguish clearly between two very different things. First, the actual suffering and wickedness involved in the events you have described. That suffering and that wickedness properly call forth from us compassion and indignation. These are warm emotions. There is nothing cold about them. But there is a second thing presented in your story—an argument, based on evidence and directed to a conclusion; namely that there is no good God. This is a piece of reasoning. And reasoning must not call out in us either compassion or

188

indignation—or indeed any other emotion. No, reasoning must properly call us to cold intellectual analysis which scrupulously separates truth from falsehood, valid deductions from illogicalities. You have the right to expect me to weep at a story of misery. You have the right to expect me to apply myself coldly to analysis of a theoretical argument. But you have no right to get me weeping at a story of misery and then, under cover of the tears, to palm off an argument on to me unexamined, with the plea that it would be indecent to stop crying in order to scrutinize it."

Jago, who was sufficiently shrewd to appreciate a good argument, even when it was at his own expense, took this with good humour.

"O.K. I see your point. Though I don't agree with your case as a whole."

"The sufferings of the innocent can be a great stumbling-block to good men," the canon said quietly. "God's ways are very mysterious, but we must not exercise our brains to make them more mysterious still. There remains some uncertainty about the facts of this case. What particular kind of heroism or sanctity Miriam Wadham may have been able to achieve in that perverted world we do not know. It is impossible to speculate about the degree of virtue sustained or the degree of degeneracy tasted. But at least we know this. That there are veins of generosity, compassion, and charity, that can be opened up by contact with the pimp and the ponce and the brothel-haunter which would never be touched in the ordinary course of suburban life.

"Every environment, even the most horrible, offers

its own special opportunities for virtue as well as for vice. We must not concentrate on the latter and totally ignore the former. To be thrown into an environment wholly unfavourable to sanctity in its externals is not all spiritual loss. And to be thrown into an environment which is to all appearances favourable to sanctity is not all spiritual gain. By no means. The harlot has opportunities for self-conquest unknown to the rector's wife. And the rectory offers temptations unknown in the brothel.

"We must not become so blind as to forget these things. For our Lord found better company in Mary Magdalene than in the pharisee who invited him to dinner. God knows, I've seen expensively educated deans in their deaneries and bishops in their palaces of whom one could say: It had been better for their souls had they been brought up in the slum or the stews. For then their grossest sins would never have grown to such a consuming potency."

The unconventionality of this judgment and the pressure of the canon's sincerity touched Jago deeply, and for the first time he began to give a little ground.

"Perhaps I'm up the pole," he said, relaxing. "Perhaps I'm warped." He sighed. "Well, if I am, it's not surprising. I've had some rough luck in my time. People talk about happiness: and I suppose it exists for them. But for me—no. I've learned to do without it."

"I'm sorry," the canon said quietly, sympathetically.

Roland tried to ease the newly-gathering tension.

"Come, come, Jago. Things aren't all that bad."

But Jago continued to address the canon.

"I've had a pretty raw deal from life."

"Illness?" the canon probed, sensing that Jago wanted to say more.

"No, not that. Just a dismal let-down, where you least expect it."

"It can be very hard," the canon said.

"It can." There was feeling in Jago's voice. "Though I suppose it's a common enough story these days. I was a fool to be taken in. It was eight years ago exactly. I was teaching in Haliwyke at the time. I met the girl who seemed to be right for me, and we married. Two years later we left Haliwyke and came to Delphwick. And within a year after that—one year—my wife went off with a fellow called Spruice. I had to divorce her. She left me no choice. Besides, in a way I relished it. For Spruice would rather have kept her without the marriage lines. I know his type. You may have heard of him. He owns the Royal Hotel and the Gables café."

"Oh," said the canon. He was taken aback.

"I was a fool, I suppose," Jago went on. "Mildred was a good deal younger than me. It didn't work."

"No." The canon was deeply preoccupied.

"Mind you," said Jago, rising from his seat as though he now intended to leave, "I'm not all that bitter with Mildred now. How could I be? She's put herself in such an awful mess. Spruice did marry her; but it meant nothing. He didn't stick to her for eighteen months. I believe there's talk of a divorce there now."

"Yes," said the canon. "I've heard something about it."

After Jago had left, the canon still remained.

"Jago surprised you, I think, with his murky past."

"Yes," the canon said.

"You don't know the Spruices?"

"No. But I've read of them in the paper; and I've heard something of their case."

There was a finality here. Obviously the canon was not going to say more. Then why had he lingered?

"Matrimony is a solemn business," he said heavily.

Roland's eyes widened. This was it. The canon wanted to know. Very well then, Why shouldn't he?

"It's funny you should say that. I'm just beginning to contemplate matrimony myself—remotely of course."

The canon nodded gravely.

"Julia?"

"I think I'm falling in love with her. You have a kind of interest in her. It seems only right to tell you."

"I was afraid so."

Roland received these words unsurely. How was he to take them? They sounded not quite grave, not quite ironic.

Realization came with a sudden rush. It shook Roland to the roots.

"Oh . . . You think Julia ought not to marry?"

"I have wondered whether she would."

"You mean, she ought to become a nun or something?"

The canon sighed.

"I have always hoped that she might discover a vocation."

"I see."

The two stared at each other in silence. It was plain

to Roland that he had trampled upon a dream long nourished.

"You think," Roland faltered, "she is more likely to, if I leave her alone?"

The canon remained impassive. Yet what could he say, except that he did indeed think that?

"I never thought of that," Roland went on. "Ought I to have done so?"

The canon shook his head.

"It is not our business to determine other people's vocations for them."

"Yet you say you've always had this in mind for Julia?"

"It *is* my business to cultivate the soil in which vocations may grow."

"I see."

Roland did not want to say any more. The canon had given him something to think about. He had no intention of thanking him for the gift.

"One can't do much more than that," the canon said. "I, as a priest, ought not to do less."

And what about me, as a marrying man? Roland thought. But he said nothing.

9

SOMETIMES ACUTE personal crises steal upon men un-
awares. A light touch on the shoulder, a word in the
ear, and the bottom drops out of one's familiar world.
And once the bottom has gone, the rest of the contents
slither after it. Yet, as Canon Kirkbride was so fond of
observing, it is too easy to talk of the impact of tragedy;
too easy to gather into a prose generalization the
jumbled, inconclusive pains of the thing itself—first
the cracking, then the crumbling, then the landslide,
as the long-settled fabric of customary thought and
habit disintegrates. After the event, of course, one can
beat the experience into shape, and perhaps philoso-
phize about it. But the living through it takes place at
a level where the intellect fumbles, where the only
wisdom is the wisdom of the will, and where the disciplined heart is a better anchorage than the sharpened
brain.

When the door bell rang on that drab January evening, Howard went to answer it, little suspecting that
within a few minutes a quite different Howard Prentice would walk the same corridor in the opposite
direction. And yet even those words, he would have
said, put the matter too clearly, too positively. Perhaps
it would be more to the point to say that within a few

minutes there was no longer a Howard Prentice at all. For up to that moment Howard Prentice consisted of certain hopes, desires, fears, and uncertainties, united around a single centre of rather hazy purposefulness. And after that moment these hopes, desires, fears, and uncertainties were numbed by a sudden paralysis, and all sense of purpose, however vague, was swallowed up in a black bewilderment.

It was Conrad Spruice.

"Come in," Howard said.

"No, I won't come in."

Howard stared at the uncompromisingly static figure. That Conrad should have called at all was surprising. That he should choose to talk at the door was astonishing.

"I only want a few words with you."

There was no confidence in Conrad's voice: there was neither assertiveness nor display; there was not even an outward semblance of grip or thrust. This represented a total destruction of the familiar Conrad Spruice, and it ought to have prepared Howard for the impending obliteration of Howard Prentice.

Howard stared at the awkward, deflated figure, as his hands plunged nervously into his overcoat pockets and then jumped nervously out again. Something was very wrong.

"I don't know how you stood—how you stand with Mildred." There was a tremor in Conrad's voice which Howard found positively unnerving. What was his game now?

"I think you do," Howard said.

Conrad looked down at the ground without replying,

waiting for Howard's sarcasm to evaporate, as though it were in bad taste. As indeed it proved to be. The meekness of Conrad's silence was totally out of character. It seemed to lift the scene out of this world.

"It's bad news," Conrad said with an effort, and Howard suddenly felt ashamed. "She's in Delphwick Hospital."

"What is it?" Howard imagined a sudden attack of appendicitis, or something of the kind.

Conrad's hands went to his pockets again, and he turned sideways from the door, to gaze into the next garden.

"This afternoon, in Towngate. She was crossing the road. There was a bus and a motor-cycle—I don't know what happened. But she was hit pretty badly."

"Can I go and see her?"

It seemed to Howard the least he could do. And for a moment, in the silence, he pictured himself approaching a fresh white hospital bed, laden with a bunch of flowers.

"She was very badly injured," Conrad said, still trying to isolate himself from Howard's presence by staring into the distance. And there was the unmistakable bleakness of the grave in his voice.

Neither of the two moved. Conrad waited for Howard to say the word.

"Dead?"

"Yes."

Howard heard then the long whistle of a train, sustained through the darkness like the cry of a living creature; and he never afterwards heard a train whistle at night without re-living momentarily that halting of significant existence which the news of Mildred's death imposed. Before the magnitude of the spoken fact and the lingering mechanical cry Conrad had shrunk to the dimensions of a shivering waif; and Howard felt slighter than he. The stroke stripped them bare of futile passions; and when these were gone, there seemed to be nothing left of either of them.

"She never regained consciousness," Conrad said, trying at least to limit the scope of her suffering. "I must go. I have others to see." And he turned away.

Howard stood there aimlessly in the light drizzle and watched him go. He was not conscious of conflict or tension; not even of pain. He was not aware of an obdurate fact which he had to digest nor of a deprivation which he had to resign himself to. He was aware only of emptiness at the centre, where purpose and desire are born. Blows strike, and one reels under them: but this was not like that. It was a sudden erosion of the identity, and he looked in vain for a stricken, staggering self. Then unconscious habit directed him back to his room.

He leaned over and looked down on Mildred's face. Never had he seen her features so tranquil, her mouth so untroubled by peevishness or passion. Even in the earliest days of their relationship, when they could meet without quarrelling and look at each other without resentment, even then her face had never been quite free from the furtive shadow of uncertainty. She had rarely looked at him steadily: and sometimes, when their faces met, her uneasy brown eyes had seemed to search his emotional resources, like a frightened dog lost in a wood. Now she had given herself utterly, beyond the reach of insecurity. All her waywardness and fitfulness were lost in the mellow steadiness of repose.

Howard turned from the coffin, closed his eyes for a moment, then left the room. At the door he was met by the frail old lady who had proclaimed herself Mildred's mother. It was odd that Howard had never previously thought of Mildred as having a mother. Her freshly discovered existence was somehow an additional disturbance in an already painful situation. She gave him an uncomfortable feeling that he had injured her.

"I think I shall take a walk," Howard said, and added evasively, "until it's time."

She nodded. Words did not come easily to her this morning. No doubt she understood Howard's desire not to join the company of near-relations and family friends now chatting together in low tones in the next room. Her worn old face distressed him. It was a wrinkled caricature of Mildred's face. Howard lowered his eyes from looking at her. He tended now to think of Mildred, not as he had last seen her, but as he had first seen her three years ago. And no doubt Mildred's mother cast her mind back too—to much earlier days, when Mildred was a long-legged, brown-eyed girl, with a bicycle and a satchel, and nothing more worrying than homework to trouble her. In those days there must have been a father too—though Howard had never heard any mention of him on Mildred's lips—and no doubt he had hoped for good things for his growing daughter; a career, perhaps; more likely, a good husband and a happy little family circle.

Mildred's mother opened the outer door for Howard and looked searchingly up the road.

"I shan't forget the time," Howard said, doing his best to set her mind at rest about the morning's formalities.

"I expect my son-in-law will be here soon," she said, before closing the door.

This use of the word "son-in-law" made Howard close his eyes in mute resistance to what it was supposed to convey. That Conrad should be called "son-in-law" by this dear, down-trodden, sad-faced woman at the door of her white and red little box of a semi-detached —somehow this was grotesque. He could not conceive of Conrad as existing in that kind of relationship with anyone, least of all with a woman of such prosaic social background as Mildred's mother. But, having digested this shock, he found himself trying to digest the fact that it *was* a shock. Why was it unthinkable that acquaintances of his, like Conrad or Roger, should exist in ordinary connections with the ordinary people of the earth? Why should they not have mothers-in-law in council housing estates, tucked away under red tiles and behind grained doors? Was this incongruity a judgment upon his peculiar circle of acquaintances? Or upon the ordinary folk, like this innocent old dear with her red eyes and lined cheeks?

He walked out of the little estate into the main road, a busy thoroughfare noisy with traffic. There was a thin mist, which added to the depression and seemed appropriate for the funeral. The wide pavements of Haliwyke High Street stretched forward, straight as a die, flanked by shop-windows. And this was what Mildred had in mind on those rare occasions when she spoke of "going home" for the week-end. He sauntered along, glad to be away from the oppressive atmosphere of the housing estate, where the clusters of identical houses, painfully humdrum and aggressively stable in their ordinariness, seemed to challenge—even accuse him. For they belonged to the world of Mildred's mother, with her tired, injured eyes and her silent reproachfulness. They represented a life of pedestrian domesticity from which Mildred had escaped, only to be corrupted (was that the right word?) by the likes of Conrad and himself.

Corrupted, and then destroyed. Brought back to her frail, ingenuous mother, with the light for ever gone out of her eyes. Howard frowned and pressed his teeth together. Why should these inconsequential thoughts come to trouble him, as though he had shared in bringing about her death? For no death could have been more meaningless—and none more natural to twentieth-century urban existence. Mildred had tried to cross Towngate hurriedly in front of a stationary bus, seizing the opportunity provided by a sudden break in the stream of traffic coming from her left, and failing to notice a motor-cyclist sweeping past the standing bus on her right. The coroner had exonerated the cyclist, who indeed had done what he could on the wet, slippery road, and had then given the court an impromptu lecture on pedestrian crossings.

Of course no mention of Mildred's private life had been made at the inquest. It was irrelevant. Yet, for Howard, the story of her broken marriages and her affairs hung like a shadow over the proceedings. An unhappy pattern had worked itself out to a tragic conclusion; and he seemed to be involved in the guilt of it all. He could not shake off this strange feeling of partial responsibility for Mildred's death. Yet, at the same time, he told himself that it was utterly irrational and sentimental to see himself mixed up in the disaster. It flew in the face of fact and logic. There was no causal connexion between his liaison with Mildred and her untimely death.

Yet still he felt inextricably involved. He had played his part in the total moral disorder of the burnt-out life. He had been at her side in the undirected course which had careered to this dismal termination. The very termination itself seemed to fix him in a strange alliance with her own weakness against her better self. For Howard began to indulge a very odd notion; a kind of fabricated superstition, it seemed to him at first. Mildred was the only woman he had had sexual relations with. Now that she was dead, he felt, more than ever, that he was furtively bound to her by this fact. Indeed, he felt that his relationship with Mildred was somehow more firm and unshakable now than it would have been had she still lived. Her death seemed to make it impossible finally and irrevocably to clinch the break they had agreed upon six months ago. The agreement was now an unratified treaty, hanging for the rest of his life in ineffectual suspense.

Odder still, Howard began to imagine an illogical, and even unchronological, connexion between Mildred's death and his failure to keep Elizabeth. Mildred's death bound him retrospectively to her over the period preceding it; the period during which he had tried to hustle Elizabeth into marriage. All this, he tried to assure himself, was highly irrational. Yet it came to him forcefully in the form of disquieting questions. How could he have hoped to break finally away from Mildred when this had been hanging over her? How could he have dared to think of marrying another while Mildred was walking through her last mortal weeks towards her death? He felt like one taking part in a dramatic tragedy, who had tried to run away from the theatre in the interval before the calamitous last act.

The more he brooded, the more uncomfortable he felt. To say that he felt guilty would be an understatement. With all his heart he wished that Mildred and he had never been more than friends to each other. That was guilt certainly. But he also wished that he had not been caught by the catastrophe in the act of escaping from her. It was like ratting as the ship went down, when he was himself the cause of the ship's foundering. In some perverse way he was both guilty of guilt, and guilty of treachery to his own guilt.

How did Canon Kirkbride's teaching about penitence apply to a case like this? Suppose he wished to repent his contribution to Mildred's general misfortune, then whom should he crawl to? Whom had he wronged except Mildred herself? Her mother perhaps. But he could scarcely go to her and say "I'm sorry", opening up a sordid chapter in Mildred's life of which she was perhaps quite ignorant. There had been no injury to Conrad. It was not a case of wife-stealing. Conrad had lost all interest in Mildred long before he came along. Indeed there was every reason to suspect that Conrad had brought the two of them together with the precise intention that they should have an affair. No. There was no one from whom he ought to ask forgiveness.

On second thoughts, Howard knew this was wrong. Canon Kirkbride had spoken of God's forgiveness. As though God were personally injured by offences committed against all and sundry. This suggested in God a capacity for being injured which Howard had never associated with divinity. On this reasoning, God must spend a good deal of his time—or his eternity—in being gratuitously injured. Perhaps he did. If so, he had cast himself for a rather dismal rôle in the management of the universe. How could an offence against another be an offence against God?

The canon, of course, had the answer to that one too. God planned a way of living for all men generally and for each man in particular, and, when you didn't fit in, you offended him. Presumably, what he planned for Howard Prentice did not include falling in love with Conrad's wife. And in that case he had to repent an offence against God's will for him—and his will for Mildred. Howard shuddered physically to see how a train of thought which had begun in defence of his innocence had terminated in acceptance of his guilt. He was not a blind fool. The turns in the argument which had directed his thinking to this unpleasant conclusion were of course casually remembered fragments of Canon Kirkbride's conversation. Why should he give such weight to these fragments of partisan propaganda? Was there a subjective psychological explanation—that the canon's little exhortations had caught up on him at a time of emotional and nervous strain, when his rational resistance to suggestion was at a low ebb? Or was there a deeper, religious explanation—that the will of a scheming, all-seeing God was making itself known to him through the canon's voice?

Howard shook his head, in the hope that he might shake it empty of superstitious nonsense as a dog shakes water from its body. He glanced rapidly at his surroundings; the radio shop, the grocer's, the tobacconist's, and then, oddly, the dirty little corrugated-iron chapel with its cheap little placard—'Lo, I am with you always, even unto the end of the world!' He was back again with a jolt at the idea of the interfering God; the omniscient God who can see through walls and ceilings; the supernatural Third Party present to every relationship; the inescapable shadow in the background. He had been introduced to this menacing figure by Canon Kirkbride, when he first called to see him about getting baptized, and now he was in danger of finding himself unable to shake the spectre off. Presumably that was what people meant by "conversion". Some pious friend comes to supper one evening, and brings God along with him. Once inside, the uninvited Guest forgets to go. The host is trapped in a moment of genial expansiveness or sensitive susceptibility, and he finds himself with a permanent Lodger till kingdom come. And the more polite and patient he is with the new Resident, the greater his demands become, until he is running the whole show; and you get fellows like Canon Kirkbride, who haven't got any private life and can scarcely call their souls their own.

Howard shrugged his shoulders as he walked. It was not possible to get rid of the idea by ridiculing it. Inwardly he had felt guilty, and he had sought to explore the feeling in the secret hope that he might dissolve it. But now, having explored, he no longer merely felt guilty; he knew that he was guilty. He had tried to play counsel and witness at his own trial, but he had finished up in the dock, and the verdict had gone against him. It was not enough to say that he had offended Mildred—though of course he had. Indeed it was just as true to say that Mildred had offended him. There was a guilt which he shared with Mildred, and with Conrad. The guilt bound them together in offence against something. It was not the law of the land, for they were law-abiding citizens. Nor was it the code of their contemporaries generally which passed judgment upon them; for they were no worse, if no better, than the general run of the people in their particular social group. Besides, it took something more than broken laws and codes to pump into the system this distressing sense of being, not just wrong, but unworthy. There was a personal judgment upon them. There was an injured Person. People like Elizabeth and Canon Kirkbride were on the other side of the fence, not merely in their obedience to a code, but more essentially in their attachment to a Person.

There was a corollary to all this, which stared Howard in the face. Mildred had not been annihilated. That was unthinkable. It would have been impossible to feel thus bound to an extinguished personality. Besides, he could not endure the idea that her life-story, which was now assuming for him a tremendous and tormenting significance, had for her evaporated in meaninglessness. Still less could he bear the notion that she survived elsewhere unchanged or unchanging. If her death brought to him, who still lived, this sense of their common guilt before an offended Person, could it have done less for her? Was he unwillingly enlightened, while she, the agent and the cause of his enlightening, remained in the dark? If there was sense and meaning in the scheme of things, this could not be. All that he groped after she now saw clearly for herself.

It is difficult to record convincingly and in full force experiences of rare illumination which play a large part in shaping or changing the whole course of men's lives. A thought came to Howard at this point, whose influence he was never afterwards able to escape. It issued naturally and cogently from the train of his reflection, yet its impact was tremendous. For it seemed to throw light into previously unexplored corners of his mind and upon previously uninterpreted passages of his life, so that it assumed the character of a revelation. It was a thought which he would formerly have found crude and indigestible. Yet, at this moment, for all its shocking unfamiliarity, he found it irresistible, unrejectable. It was this. There is a deep connexion, he told himself, between the fact that I feel more closely bound to Mildred than ever, and the fact that I am burdened with a sense of guilt and teased with the image of an offended Judge. The connexion is direct. We are more closely bound because we two now share the same new sense of our common guilt. And the connexion is causal. For the origin of this new illumination lies with her, beyond the grave. She sees our guilt: it is brought home to her: she acknowledges an offended Judge. And

206

she is not content to leave me in outer darkness. Her guilt, her awakening, and her acknowledgment reach into time and draw me to a share in her changed condition. Her death involves me in her own new life. It has already become a part of a pattern which I can either accept or reject. But, if I reject it, I reject God. For this is what it means to come face to face with the will of God.

Of course it was not as clear as that. It did not break into Howard's brain in sentences. It grew. Indeed in later life Howard found it impossible to extricate clearly the revelation, as it then occurred to him, from the accretions which afterwards gathered round it. Nevertheless, its fundamental character did not change. It was from the start a fumbling, groping recognition of a great truth. For the first time in his life he recognized the relationship between the dead and the living. For the first time he saw death as something more meaningful than mere extinction. For the first time he was aware, inwardly and not just cerebrally aware, of a pattern and a Purposer; conscious of a personal demand from God himself. He knew himself entangled in a common guilt and, more mysteriously, involved in the penitence and the prayers of another. It is not to be expected that the meaning of these awakenings should have been immediately apparent, except in a sketchy, half-realized fashion. But the concrete experience was more moving to him, for all the blurring of the outlines in the brain, than the mind's subsequent clarifications and enrichments of it. Mildred had died and had become different. Somewhere she was helping to pay the price of changing him too. Careless and meaningless as it seemed at first to be, her death had now been made an instrument to touch him. This was its part in the divine plan for him. Mildred acquiesced and put him eternally in her debt.

As Howard returned to the house, he paid more attention to his surroundings. And the sudden focussing of his attention on the brightly-lit shop-windows, the passing traffic, and the hurrying women with their shopping-baskets, produced an experience which was new to him, though perhaps commonplace enough in the lives of many. Certainly he had read of something like it at school in the poets, though poetry had never touched him much. He felt that his immediate surroundings belonged to an unreal world, ultimately less substantial than the world of his inner life, where thought flung his newly-awakened sensitivities against the fact of death and the fact of human sin. More, not only did the urban surroundings seem comparatively unreal; they seemed alien too. They were less close to him, less involved in the issue of his well-being, than the living claims of a woman who had died three days ago. For the shops and the factories and the buses belonged to the world of her pale, spiritless corpse, which would soon be rotting in the earth. But he himself belonged to the world of her present prayers and living penitence, the world of her unextinguished claims upon the Judge and the judged.

There was a line of sombre funeral cars in the road outside the house, when he returned. It gave the street a solemn, strangely static air. Suddenly it felt like Sunday. But the scene did not move him as he had expected to be moved. For these cars too belonged to an alien, unreal world, whose grip upon him had been lightened by Mildred's death. As he turned into the house, an ironically unwelcome sensation occurred to him, outrageous, it seemed, and wicked: for he sensed underneath the black-suited sorrow an impulse to peaceful resignation so warming and sweetening that he wanted to call it happiness.

Howard was given a lift back to Delphwick in Roger's car. Conrad sat beside Roger in the front seat and Howard sat alone in the back. All were, in their different ways, relieved to know that the funeral formalities were now behind them. When they turned left from the main Haliwyke-Garton road, Roger began to gather the maximum speed in preparation for the long ascent up to the moor top, and Conrad, unexpectedly, tried to restrain him.

"Steady, old man. Surely you've had a lesson to-day. I shan't be in the mood for speed again for a long time."

The acceleration was increased.

"I feel just the opposite," Roger said.

"Feel what you like. You've got two passengers. And I for one don't want my head bashed in against the roof."

"Why not? What better way to leave the human scene? No long-drawn-out misery. One stunning blow, and it's all over."

"Don't be a bloody fool," Conrad said, really angry, as Roger overtook a lorry with a blind bend immediately ahead. "You have the right to feel suicidal: but you're heading for manslaughter."

209

"I've always thought a great thing about mechanical progress is the enormous increase it has brought in the less unpleasant ways of dying." Roger sounded only half-serious.

"All ways of dying are damned unpleasant," Conrad said.

"It's the anticipation of death which is unpleasant. But deaths in transit, by land or air, are unanticipated."

"Not in this case."

"The machine kills cleanly and unexpectedly. Provided you drive fast enough, you're unlikely to cripple yourself. You'll live in health, or you'll die."

"I prefer to live."

Conrad had calmed down, for the steeper gradient had restricted Roger's impulse to speed.

"That's not the question. We're arguing about the best way to die."

"We've had enough death for one day. For God's sake change the subject."

"By all means. There's no point in death. The rule of healthy living is to ignore it. If you foresee it every time you get into a car, you knock all the security out of life, and make life meaningless too."

Howard pondered this half-serious generalization. Did death make life meaningless? Was death given to us simply as a negation, cancelling out the significance of things? Was it given to men to be forgotten and ignored? Or was it there to determine the human attitude to life itself? Was it something which had to be taken into account in framing a rational view of things? A new simplification of his thinking occurred to him. The difference between the religious and the irreligious view of life was that the former took death into account. For when he had seriously taken Mildred's death into account, he had been forced back upon a religious picture of life. It seemed that all irreligious views of life relied upon forgetfulness of death. But if death were total and final extinction, then Mildred was now obliterated, and all thought of her as a real personality was so much anachronistic day-dreaming. One could not have it both ways. Either she was simply a past failure, now annihilated; or she was still an existing creature, changed as he too must one day be changed. Everything of importance which he had felt to-day assured him that life was made more meaningful by death. Death provided the one inescapable revelation of the difference between good and evil.

"Did you see that screwed up little fellow who walks like the leaning tower of Pisa?" Conrad asked.

"The one who went off in the Ford Prefect?" Apparently Roger had noticed him.

"Yes, that's the fellow. That's Bingley."

"Bingley?"

"You know, Mildred's first husband."

"Good God! He looks fifty."

"But he isn't. It's just premature decay. It started in his teens."

"Can't think what Mildred saw in him. Not her type at all, I should have said."

"Rather mean, I think." Conrad swelled visibly. "The fellow refuses to speak to me. I can't think why. It isn't as though I did him any harm. *De mortuis* and all that, but you know, I did rather lift a load off his back."

Conrad hummed. Howard, in the back seat, wished it were as easy, as Conrad seemed to imply, to divest oneself of metaphorical loads on the back. Brooding, he was suddenly conscious of Conrad's shining spectacles and moon-like face.

"Have you gone to sleep there?"

"No. I was just thinking."

"It's the worst thing you could possibly do."

"Leave him alone," said Roger, "he's moody."

"I don't blame him. That service gave me the creeps. Why can't they do something to bring it up to date? All that about dust to dust and ashes to ashes is such frightful nonsense. Poor Mildred was never dust and ashes, whatever else she may have been."

"It's poetry, my dear fellow."

"Well, I hate it. And why must these parsons keep dragging God into the business?"

"It's what they're paid to do."

"Someone ought to pay them a bit more to leave him out of it. It goes against the grain at funerals."

"We have to put the blame on somebody."

"It's hypocrisy."

"No doubt," said Roger, "but if it makes people happy, where's the harm? Let's have a bit more hypocrisy, if it gives people what they want and makes them feel nice inside."

Howard winced. So they would say of him, if he began to evince a taste for religion. The price of getting what he wanted. Elizabeth purchased by a sudden conversion. Was it as simple and crude as that? Were all his inner doubts and questions subtly motivated by the desire to enter a sphere of life from which he was excluded—a sphere which contained the inaccessible Elizabeth? Was he seeking the truth, or merely seeking a wife? Did he want a religion unless he got Elizabeth too?

He knew that in honesty his case could not be analysed thus. Indeed he would have been happier if the religious question had been mainly an issue between himself and Elizabeth. But it was not at all that. It was an issue between himself and Mildred. That was what made it so uncomfortably real—so inseparable from the fact of death and the fact of evil. It was not entangled with his possible future happiness; it was tied up with his inescapable past sins. He did not want a God now who would just present him with Elizabeth. He wanted a God who would wipe out the evil that had been between Mildred and himself. If only his problem could have been an issue with the living, instead of an issue with the dead! If only he could feel himself bound in obligation to the prayers of a future bride, instead of to the prayers of a past mistress! If only he could be concerned, even distressed, about something on this side of the grave! He wanted nothing more desperately than to be shut up comfortably within the span of mortal life again. But doors had been opened on existence beyond its boundaries. And it was Mildred who had gone through. No doubt Canon Kirkbride had helped to open the doors; he and even Elizabeth herself to some extent. But it was Mildred who had made use of them, to involve him for ever in her doings on the other side.

IO

It was Canon Kirkbride, of course, who had suggested to Roland the idea of making a Retreat. The suggestion was so mixed up in Roland's mind with the canon's rather furtive pressure against an engagement with Julia that he felt he could not decently ignore it. It would be resisting the canon openly on two distinct fronts at once if he made no Retreat and yet got engaged to Julia. Vaguely, at the back of his mind, Roland felt that, if he made the Retreat, then he would have appeased the canon sufficiently. It would then be possible to ask Julia to marry him without feeling that he was snubbing Father Kirkbride.

Thus it was that he came to Holy Trinity House for a Lenten week-end at the beginning of March. It was a Beginners' Retreat, strictly reserved for first-timers and, to begin with, most of the retreatants spent a great deal of mental energy in staring in astonishment at themselves for being there at all. When they were not mentally preoccupied thus, they were staring in even greater astonishment at the permanent residents of the place. As the interminable series of offices in the chapel flowed by, few of the visitors could for long put away the persistent question—How was it possible for men to live permanently like this, day after day, year after year?

The first experience of seeing the life of a religious community and sharing briefly in its withdrawal from the world inevitably makes a great impact upon the mind and the emotions. Everything was strange with a flavour of strangeness never to be tasted again. Everything was unclassifiable; especially the peculiar feel of the main house itself—the odd blend of Victorian architecture with ascetic furnishings, and the incongruously ornate statues and pedestals greeting one at the turnings of staircases, on corridor window-ledges, and in alcoves designed originally for clocks, decanters, or umbrella stands. In the Retreat House the rather uncomfortable little band seated themselves self-consciously at the bare refectory tables, too obsessed with the absorbing novelty of eating without speaking, to pay much attention to the purpose of their silence. The ingenuity required in order to get hold of the salt without asking for it was itself a preoccupation which left them with little ear for the voice of one of the fathers, who read to them from a modern translation of the New Testament. Then Roland remembered for a long time afterwards the peculiar loneliness of the little bedroom in the newest wing of the Retreat House, a modern addition whose construction was like that of any residential dormitory designed to hold people living sociably together, and whose purpose was to keep them superficially apart.

Yet the impact of the external surroundings was slight indeed compared with the impact of one or two moments of revelation by which Roland was touched on the nerve already made sore by Canon Kirkbride. One such revelation came in an address by Father Charles who was conducting the retreat. Father Charles was a sleek, dark-haired little man who looked like a monk only because he was wearing the right clothes. He was a fluent speaker with an expressively flexible face which riveted the attention of those he addressed. Perhaps this was not quite so great an advantage as it might appear. Roland for one was sometimes too interested in watching the way the cheeks and eyes moved with the movement of the mouth to notice exactly what was being said. Roland had noted the same accomplished facial flexibility in action when insurance agents had tried to interest him in a new policy. He had found himself admiring their technique when they would have preferred him to be calculating the advantages of what they offered. However, the retreatants listened attentively to Father Charles through a series of talks which gradually led them to explore their own souls by the light of his exhortations. There was a good deal about penitence and self-examination, a good deal about contrition and perseverance, about resistance to besetting temptations, and about the dangers of apathy. And, of course, running like a thread through the whole series of talks, was the theme of self-surrender; the necessity for reliance upon the grace and guidance of God at every point in the progress through the Christian life.

This was not new to Roland. Canon Kirkbride had been at great pains to explain to him the peculiar and so-much-misunderstood quality of the Christian ethic, with its centre in total submission to the will of God.

But suddenly, in the last of Father Charles's addresses, a new deduction was drawn from all this, which hit Roland with the force of a thunderbolt. For once he forgot the dim chapel, the lavish sprinkling of sanctuary lamps, the incongruous religiosity of his twentieth-century urban companions in this hidden world, and even the shiny, rubber-like foldings and ripplings of Father Charles's face. For every word seemed to carry a rebuke directed at him alone.

"Most of you are young," Father Charles said, with just a hint of justifiable envy. "You have your careers before you. You face, perhaps, the choice of working at home or moving elsewhere, maybe abroad. Perhaps you face the choice between this career and that. Maybe you have before you a choice in more strictly personal matters—to marry or not to marry; to give yourself to the building of a home, or to give yourself to some work which you could more fruitfully perform as a single man. I want to speak especially to those of you who are still not irrevocably committed, by past or present circumstances, to a determined pattern of life. If you have already said to yourself, 'I shall work hard for promotion in the office, or the factory; I shall settle down in Delphwick, or Frond, or wherever it may be; I shall marry and find a nice little house on the outskirts—'; if you have said any of these things, ask yourself now: Was the decision made under the guidance of God? Was it made prayerfully? Was it made in honest openness to the will of God? Was it made reflectively and devoutly? Did you first submit your plans to God and wait patiently to hear whether his voice had any special directions for you? Or have you made your life's decisions with heart and ears closed to the voice of God? Have you made these decisions in obedience or in selfishness, in patience or in wilfulness, in self-giving or in self-seeking?

"Some of us, God knows, have little power of choice in these matters. Perhaps it is one of the major curses of our civilization that many of us find ourselves fettered to a pattern of life by force of social and economic circumstances which we are powerless to modify or deflect. If that is your case, God understands. He does not expect impossibilities. He does not call you to a course of action which reason and earthly duty will not allow you to pursue. But it is easy to miscalculate the force of outside circumstances, and even to misread the claims of earthly duty. And some of us have more freedom in these matters than we should perhaps care to admit. That is why I am asking you now to examine yourselves afresh on your plans for life. In so far as the future remains open to you, use the opportunity of this quiet week-end to submit to God the desires and schemes upon which you have set your hearts. Offer them to God in unqualified submission. Offer them in prayer, openly and without reserve. Try to achieve the sincerity of self-offering which says, 'Oh God, on these things I have set my heart. Grant me thy guidance and blessing in fufilling these desires or, if it be thy will, in rooting them out. Oh God, give me the grace of obedience. Speak to me plainly in confirming my desires or in rejecting them. And grant me the strength of thy Holy Spirit, that I may be patient and grateful, even if thy will for me contradicts what I have planned and hoped for.'

"It is a hard prayer: but it never goes unanswered. This is the last movement of self-surrender. When, by penitence and absolution, God has cleansed you from sin, then is the time to complete your self-offering by giving yourself without reserve to whatever God wills for you in the future. You remember the prodigal son? On his return home, penitent and ashamed, he did not claim for himself the status of a privileged son. 'Make me as one of thy hired servants.' He offered himself in unquestioning obedience. He had had enough of following his own will, which had led him from degradation to degradation, from misery to misery. All he wanted now was perfect submission to his father's will. That is the pattern of true penitence. We must seek to be the hired servants of our Father in heaven, or the self-offering of our penitence is incomplete.

"That is my last piece of advice. Before you leave this place, to return to your daily pursuits in the world, try to make this final act of self-offering in relation to the whole of your future life. Make no exceptions. Withold nothing. Say with all your heart, 'Use me as thou wilt.' It is the way of the Christian. And it is the way of peace."

Roland left the chapel in a tumult of self-scrutiny. And a silent, lightning encounter plunged him into deeper disquiet. For one of his fellow-retreatants, who had been placed in the bedroom next his own, passed by him just outside the chapel door, and nodded in momentary recognition. Roland could see that he was on the point of speaking and then he remembered the rule of silence. He smiled at his own forgetfulness, noting that Roland had recognized it. But there was certainly no need for him to speak. His expression spoke for him. He had been going to make some remark about the address. Quite plainly it had sustained and heartened him. And Roland it had plunged in distress. The very contrast between this stranger and himself underlined his difficulty. He walked away, to tread the grounds with his predicament.

He found a little summer-house, built on the wooded hill-side by the original owners of the house so as to command a view of the valley on whose slopes the estate had been laid out. It must have been a delightful view at one time, and still was, though the face of the scenery had changed. A canal, a railway line, and a main road now ran beside the river, half a mile or so away. The road was thick with traffic and there were barges on the canal. Two expanding nearby townships had crept up the valley, spreading council houses up the slopes on the far side. It would not be easy for the monks to become forgetful of the modern world in a spot like this. And to prevent their becoming forgetful of other things, someone's ingenuity had caused a ten-foot high Calvary to be erected in front of the summer-house, rising from a cairn-like heap of stones and moss. There was a little crucifix too hanging in the centre of the inner wall of the summer-house, and some grateful visitor or resident had half completed a series of coloured stations of the cross around this inner wall at eye-level. In short, the surroundings were not conducive to selfish or undisciplined day-dreaming, and Roland sat down there feeling that everything was conspiring against him.

He did not try to pray. The habit of informal prayer does not grow easily in the mature convert. Moreover he was half-afraid to pray; afraid of the kind of divine guidance which prayer might bring upon him. He had scarcely reached the stage of asking himself, Can I face this or that? He was simply afraid of opening himself up to the unknown—overcome with dread at the prospect of offering himself whole-heartedly to a future that was not anchored in his familiar hopes and dreams.

There were two ways in which Father Charles's appeal had touched him—in relation to his professional career, and in relation to his private life. He was one of those especially addressed by Father Charles, one quite young and free enough to be able to submit his career in self-offering to God. There was nothing, nothing at all, to prevent him from opening up his working life as a new book. He could cut out of grammar-school teaching and tackle something more arduous. He could go abroad, work in a school for delinquents, for cripples, for near-imbeciles; perhaps even get ordained or, worse still, join a religious community.

And, more grievous than all this, he was asked to submit to God in perfect openness his desire to marry Julia. Moreover it was not possible for him to offer this desire with a tolerable confidence at the back of his mind that God would pat him on the back and tell him to go ahead. On the contrary, any sneaking conviction that he was by God's direction Julia's future husband seemed to have been nailed by Canon

Kirkbride. It was incompatible with what he had gleaned from the canon's divinations.

"Make me as one of thy hired servants." That was to be his prayer—his especially because he was a prodigal, brought back into the family after wandering in the waste land of scepticism and faithlessness. And the hired servant, if he is loyal and honourable, does not begin his career of service by making love to the daughter of the house. He waits on the Father's will: the completeness of his submission is the measure of his penitence. And where the will of the Father is not clear, he waits in patience, asking nothing for himself. Precisely because he is the prodigal, freely reinstated, he stakes no claim.

Through all Roland's arguments with himself there ran a train of thought which he found it difficult to explain clearly even to himself. He saw that he had been for a long time a fugitive from his Father's house. And he felt the need for some corresponding act of distinctive service now that he had been welcomed home. It was not that he thought of himself as making a special act of appeasement or atonement. He had been too thoroughly instructed by Canon Kirkbride to allow the idea that any act of his could justify his former disobedience. But, at the very back of his mind, the sense of this especial need hung like a shadow. It was not that his long neglect of God had to be compensated for. Rather a special grace had been given him in the forgiveness of this sin, and it called for a response of service and sacrifice. It was not *demanded* of him. It was neither asked nor required. And that was why he had to make it. Because it could be pure gratitude—the free impulse of the free soul, untouched by compulsion or obligation.

This thought loomed like a shadow. It darkened his prospects without presenting itself to him in a form clear enough to be rationalized away. Of course he could not argue with this undefinable invitation. It was not even able to be expressed adequately in intellectual terms. At first the mere awareness that he ought to make no claim upon Julia, it grew to the stature of a positive call for sacrifice. And yet even the word "call" is too strong and clear a word to describe this haunting darkness. It was the shadow of his own creaturehood, bearing down upon him with the invitation to bury himself in its blackness and bite the dust it darkened.

"O God," he prayed, "grant me thy grace, not only to give what thou dost ask, which is duty and obedience, but to give also what thou dost not ask, which is love." No sooner had he said these words than he began to wonder whether he had spoken heresy, or even nonsense. There could be no higher service than to do the will of God. Was it then blasphemy to talk of giving what God had not asked? No, because the finest gratitude was to give what was neither asked nor expected: and gratitude could never be blasphemy. To give more than was asked; that was love. But, if it was not asked, how could it be in accordance with God's will?

Does God will that we should do more than he asks? Does he silence his own demand, so that he can will our undemanded giving?

Roland shook his head in the loneliness. He was beginning to talk nonsense to himself. His brain was juggling with an infinite regress. Canon Kirkbride would plough through that like a bull-dozer, no doubt. You didn't need to be a mental gymnast to understand what God was wanting of you. You only needed a bit of honesty with yourself.

His reflections were interrupted by the appearance of Brother James, strolling meditatively down the path from the House. Roland had not seen Brother James since that summer evening over two years ago when they had met in the Deans' garden. But he could see that the monk recognized him. Acting on a sudden impulse, he broke the rules and spoke.

"May I talk to you?"

"If it's important enough to justify talk."

Brother James came into the summer-house without waiting for a reply, and sat down beside him.

"How do you recognize a vocation?" Roland asked abruptly.

Brother James looked at Roland carefully, as though he were taking in more than had been said. He was quiet for a moment, and then he spoke in his most impersonal tone, staring down at the busy valley road in the distance.

"You speak as though it were something you might find lying about. You can't pick it up and weigh it against this and that."

"But you must know it when you come across it. It must have a recognizable stamp."

"Yes and no," Brother James said, and then he frowned in dissatisfaction with his own obscurity. "You see, it doesn't come into your hands like a thing presented to you externally. It grows, inside you."

Roland frowned.

"Then you must know that it is there."

Brother James shook his head.

"You will know that *something* is there. But whether you recognize it for what it is—that is a different matter. The vague dissatisfactions in the souls of men are given very different names by men of different spiritual stature. The debauchee defines his innermost hunger as a need for women; and the paranoiac feeds it as an appetite for power and influence. But the hunger at the centre of every man's being is one and the same hunger for God. And God gives this hunger its special relationship in each man to his particular gifts and his unique personality. The flowering of vocation is the discovery of this relationship."

Roland stared thoughtfully before him. Brother James struggled after greater clarity in explanation—and the struggle was reflected in his shifting glance.

"The best way of putting it," he went on, "is perhaps by a metaphor from generation. The seed of divine growth impregnates that particular body of talents and temperamental qualities which you call your personality. From that insemination vocation is conceived."

"But not necessarily born?"

Roland began to follow the drift more understandingly. This was what he wanted and dreaded to hear. Brother James's gaze became suddenly fixed.

"No. After conception there is a long and toilsome period of gestation. And before birth there is all the pain of labour."

"What you are telling me," Roland said, "means that it may be quite hard work finding out whether you have a special vocation. And I imagined that God called people with a direct message."

"God doesn't stand with a microphone in his hand. You can't discover his will for you by sitting back in a chair and switching on a short-wave receiver. You've got to work hard and pray hard. The highest vocations are sometimes discovered through the greatest toil and suffering." He raised his hand to the life-sized crucifix, rising into the blue above the surrounding bushes. "Before that solemn enthronement, there was the long agony in the garden."

"Suppose you are utterly uncertain what God wants of you?"

"In that case you must be patient: and meantime you must try not to give your self-will the benefit of the doubt."

"For how long?"

"For a life-time perhaps."

"But surely," Roland said, "that's vocational agnosticism. You can't remain in uncertainty for a life-time."

Brother James shook his head.

"Vocation covers a lot. There are vocations to the priesthood, to teaching, healing, nursing, and so on. There are vocations to parenthood and to celibacy. And some are called to plough the fields and fish on the seas, or maybe just to make meals and wash up. But it doesn't end there; for everything that God asks of man is vocation. And there is much of a different kind in the life of incarnate God which man is asked to share. Martyrdom, for instance. Martyrdom of the flesh, and martyrdom of earthly hopes and ambitions.

Those who embrace these martyrdoms are uplifted like that. That is what they share."

His hand was raised again, and his eyes were on the sombre bronze figure, black against the white cloud with the rich blackness of seaweed.

"You see," he went on, "there may be vocation to frustration or uncertainty, to unresting bewilderment before the silence of God. In these things man shares in Gethsemane, as in martyrdom he shares in Calvary."

Roland guessed that Brother James was speaking now, not just of something gleaned in the study of theology, but of something known and lived through in passion and patience. Indeed Roland saw the connexion between what Brother James said and his own rejection of the priesthood. And he was struck by the contrast between the monk's known and advertised cheerfulness and ebullience and the profound inner gravity of this implied vocation to unfulfilment. As Roland looked at his face now, he could not doubt that it was the face of a happy man, and yet his words had chilled him to the bone.

"In these negative vocations," Roland said, "if that is the right word, is there happiness?"

Brother James's face broke into a broad smile.

"Of course there is. We can offer up failure as well as success, because he is the crucified as well as the crowned. The offering of either brings peace."

II

EASTER HAD broken upon Delphwick in a blaze of long-witheld sunshine. Roland and Julia had taken a bus up to Calne Heights and were making for the moors: for, sooner or later, as the fact of Spring first seeps into the consciousness, everyone in Delphwick takes a day on the moors. By mid-day it was so unexpectedly warm that Julia had given Roland her little jacket to carry, and she walked at his side, white-bloused, green-skirted, with a freedom of movement that made him feel cumbersomely rigged out in his heavy tweeds. They covered the long climb up the Oxenshaw road before lunch, so that they could eat their sandwiches with the prospect of easier walking ahead. At the top they could see nothing but undulating moorland under a still, cloudless sky, and hear nothing except the bleat of stray sheep and the cry of the curlew. After lunch they turned from the road on to a moorland track, intending to skirt the grey peaks of Hardcliff Crags before descending into the semi-urban homeliness of the Leath valley.

Unlike Julia, Roland suffered intermittent jabs of surprise that he should be there at all. He hadn't had a day in the country with Julia before, and the present experience was not exactly his arranging. From time to time he sufficiently forgot the sun and the freshness to ask himself what it was all about. But circumstances did not encourage one to press questions of that kind. As the peacefulness of the day asked for a quiet acceptance of the earth which bred them, so too Julia's frank, unstinting responsiveness seemed to require a glad acceptance. (Gratitude, Canon Kirkbride said, involves joyful receiving. You must not be niggling with God over his gifts to you.) Where, then, in a world of sunshine, with a girl's hand there for the taking, was the place for sacrifice? Did it perhaps belong to some other sphere of life than this? (The convert, Canon Kirkbride said, sometimes rushes too headlong into self-sacrifice. That perhaps was Saint Augustine's case.) And if there was a vocation to be discovered, might it be discovered after all, not on the knees in a dim church, but on the feet under a cloudless sky? Or was that a concession to the subtle old Adam? (It may be, Canon Kirkbride said, that your great need is to discover your own ordinariness. Your particular vocation may seem very prosaic at first beside the heroic strivings of the saints and the spiritual adventures of the mystics: but, if it is your true vocation, there will be poetry in it.)

Roland chose a moment when his question would prove least embarrassing to Julia—that is, when he could not see her face. She was walking directly ahead of him, for they were on a narrow sheep-track that compelled them into single file.

"Julia, why did you ask me to come out like this to-day?"

"Because I wanted to talk to you."

"Oh."

Roland thought he understood at once. Julia was a sensible girl. That was one way of putting it. She was a responsible woman. That was a better way of putting it. She had sense, and she had sex too. And therefore he had no right to be for ever dithering at her elbow in his inconclusive way. So she was giving him his chance. Probably she had made up her mind that it was high time for finality. He had slithered between the rôles of friend and suitor long enough.

"Watch your step," Julia said, not without cause, for the undergrowth hung over the path, in patches concealing it completely. This made it necessary to concentrate on the feet, for the route had apparently been peppered with giant eggs of stone at some point in history. Embedded in the soil of the path, they raised their backs high enough to trip up the unwary.

Suddenly a very different explanation of things entered Roland's head, and it lay on his mind for some moments like a dead hand. Perhaps the idea that Julia should enter a convent was not, after all, a pipe dream of Canon Kirkbride's. Perhaps this was a real issue in her life. Perhaps she had recently come to a decision. And now she had sought this opportunity to explain to Roland, as delicately and affectionately as she could. She had understood him better than he had understood himself. She knew that he was in love with her. She knew it was going to be hard for him.

Yes, that was it. Canon Kirkbride had given him the hint clearly enough, and yet he had failed to take the warning as seriously as he should. He had been so obsessed recently with the thought of God's possible call to him that he had failed to take into account God's demand upon Julia herself. There was a rich irony in this. That he should have pondered so tortuously—and so unnecessarily—whether he was himself available for marriage, when Julia's unavailability was probably already established. And as the prospect of her self-dedication to the religious life loomed up before him, he began to sense for the first time what barrenness there might be in an existence without her.

"Julia," he blurted nervously. "I suppose you made your mind up long ago about marrying and all that?"

He was aware that the words sounded silly. But he was desperately anxious to get to grips.

"Marrying?" Julia said without turning. "How should I have made up my mind? No one has asked me."

"Oh."

Roland tried to pull himself together quickly after this sudden stab of surprise and delight.

"As yet," Julia added, without turning her head.

What then? She was exactly two feet away in an uninhabited world of silence. Roland might have taken her round the waist from behind, and breathed a word into her hair. He could have gripped her arms, and held her still, and waited without a word for the answering movement—the sudden, wilful shaking free, or the willing relaxation. 'If it is your true vocation, there will be poetry in it.' Where the vocation is, there is the poetry. But that did not mean that where the poetry is, there the vocation is too. Or did it?

At any rate they continued as they were. Though Roland wished he could have been the kind of person to have taken Julia on the thought, and not the kind to have pictured himself taking her, only then to withdraw. (Continual self-reference is bad, Canon

231

Kirkbride said, even when it takes the form of self-judgment.) For the day and the hour were a denial of self-denial. The sky and the quiet and Julia's hair, lifted by the fresh breeze, could only be denied by self-centred ingratitude. (Consciously to pursue opportunities for self-sacrifice is dangerous, Canon Kirkbride said. You will find yourself engaged in sacrifice when you ought to be pleasing someone else. A man may deny himself a cup of tea when it would be better for him to put the kettle on for his wife and himself.)

"What did they do to you at Holy Trinity House?" Julia asked. "You have been very pensive since you came back."

"There was a good deal of talk about vocation."

"Ah, I see."

"It made me wonder what I ought to do. Perhaps I may find something more adventurous than my present job."

"Not very difficult," Julia said slyly.

"No," Roland laughed. "Maybe an approved school. Or perhaps something abroad. There's Africa. It needs thinking about carefully."

"I think you are right. I should like to go abroad too."

"There are other things as well . . . You know, Julia, I've a lot to thank you for."

"I doubt it."

"Yes, I have. You must have thought me a queer type when we first got to know each other."

She remained silent.

"But I think it was your doing that Gregory brought me into touch with Canon Kirkbride."

"Yes, it was," she said.

When they reached Hardcliff Crags, they climbed
on top of one of the great grey rocks to enjoy the view.
They sat down together on Roland's spread-out rain-
coat; behind them, the rolling, hummocky moors,
receding into the skyline; before them, in the distance,
the long curve of Leath valley, the little patches of
smoke hanging over the houses like the trail left by a
train. Suddenly Julia spoke as though she had waited
all day for this moment alone.

"Going back to the retreat. Have you reached the
stage of brooding about heroic vocations, like joining a
community?"

"Brooding," Roland said. "Well, a little. But nothing very heroic."

"I thought so. I've been through the stage myself. It
passes. Unless you're one of the rare exceptions."

"There's nothing very rare about me."

"No. In that sense, I don't think there is."

The need to discover his own ordinariness. Yet the
ordinariness was charged with poetry indeed, when he
was hearing what he did hear, thus lifted literally on
top of the world. And she whom he had pursued so
long.

"Brother James had a go at me once," Julia said.
"He said that I had the makings of a nun. He told
Canon Kirkbride that he could see the spiritual life in
my eyes."

Roland was flabbergasted. That any male human
being with Brother James's vigour and comparative
youthfulness could look into Julia's eyes and solemnly

declare that he saw the spiritual life there—this was an astonishing revelation of the differences that could be between man and man.

"Of course," Julia added, "if anyone can make you think you're called to the cloister, Brother James can."

"Yes," Roland said feelingly, "you're right there."

"He makes you doubt whether you have the right to breathe or eat."

"Or marry," Roland added.

"Which shows," Julia said, "just how rightly he has chosen himself."

"But he's not a pattern for others, you would say?"

"Not for everyone."

There was silence between them. Roland stared at the hills beyond the Leath valley; the solitary knuckle of Howden Pike jerking awkwardly into the blue, and behind it the long slope of Blackmoor Edge, the boundary of this half-industrialized medley of mill and moor. Beyond it was the limestone land of white walls and smokeless valleys, where the dale farmers lived in the open with their sheep.

Julia stared too. And, without withdrawing her eyes from the distance, she began to speak again.

"Some things are just given to you. And they are so wonderful that it would be ungrateful not to accept them. They are just given, to make you happy. And you know that you have no right to say no. They are not things that could be passed on to others who are in greater need, like money or even food. They are for you alone. You can't close your eyes before them and turn away; because you know you're not meant to."

Roland did not speak; for he did not know how. And he hoped she would say more.

"Of course," she added, "you can spoil them. But you won't, so long as you remember that they have been given; that they are gifts."

And still Roland did not know what to say. Julia turned and looked at him, insisting on a reply.

"Isn't that so?" she asked.

"I think it is," Roland said, avoiding her eyes.

"But you're not sure?" she pressed.

"Well," he said, still looking down, "how do you know a gift a temptation?"

"You can see the hand of the Giver in it."

He took her own hand. Nothing more than that. He traced with his thumb the line of a tapering finger from knuckle to tip. He squeezed her palm gently, and she smiled.

"Julia."

She turned, and their eyes met. He searched their grey depths and shook his head.

"I cannot see what Brother James saw."

The eyelids flickered nervously over a surface that glistened with laughter.

"What *can* you see?"

"Only myself," Roland said, "transfigured."

A solitary curlew wheeled over them, and a single sheep cried out in the distance.

12

ON TUESDAY in Easter week Canon Kirkbride took an afternoon walk on his own for the purpose of thinking. Earlier in the day, Mr Dean, Julia's father, had phoned to say that Julia was now officially engaged to Roland Tay. This half-expected news the canon found difficult to relish wholeheartedly. And he blamed himself for this lack of enthusiasm.

Indeed, as he turned off the Haydon road to climb up through the golf links to Allerham Top, he decided that this lingering rebelliousness of his was positively sinful. For there was now no solid objective reason for believing that Julia had ever felt a vocation to the religious life. On the contrary, there was every reason for the canon to believe that his ideas on the subject had been wide of the mark. Still, there were things which the canon knew and no one else knew. In spite of everything which Julia and Roland might say to each other, he had not invented Julia's hypothetical "vocation" himself. It had come from Mrs Dean herself, on her deathbed, and that surely was what made it so real and gave it such a solemn quality. Looking back, as he had so often looked back before, to that moving occasion, he believed it almost impious to suggest that it had all meant nothing. He struck the stone wall with his walking stick as he passed.

Then suddenly he stopped, and stared hard at the grey shape of a building plastered on the grass and the sky. Once a flourishing farm-house for one of those vigorous families who worked these upland fields, it was now little better than decaying slum property, pitched incongruously on grassland that catered for suburban golf-balls and courting couples rather than for sheep and cows. The canon stared, and asked himself a piercing question. Had he been guilty of the very sin he had so often defined and clarified for others? That of presuming to know God's business better than God himself? Since the original idea came from Mrs Dean, he could not accuse himself of presumptuously hatching the take-over of a human soul. It was certainly his duty, as a priest, to pay the maximum attention to such solemn statements as Mrs Dean's. But need he have been quite so cocksure? Had he not been on the point of pushing with all the pressure of sacred authority a project which was of his own devising? Were there the seeds here of a spiritual possessiveness frightening in its potentiality?

The canon shuddered and crossed himself. God forgive me, he muttered. And keep my judgment sound, he added, quickening his stride. If I must not try to see further than God, neither must I put on blinkers. Watchfulness for vocations must not be allowed to lapse simply because there has been an error—and perhaps more than an error?—in this particular case. It was necessary to wait on God's decisions: but one had

237

to wait with open eyes. One had to look for shape and meaning.

Canon Kirkbride liked things to make a pattern. He found that, if you waited long enough, things generally did make a pattern. Events fell into place, and the divine Designer was revealed at the back of even the most discrete and fragmentary experiences. He must conclude this time that he had looked too soon and too confidently for the rounding-off of the pattern begun on Mrs Dean's death-bed. After all, the canon smiled to himself, you didn't need to have a head stuffed with sex to be able to see that Julia Dean was intensely marriageable. And presumably that was God's work too. Presumably that too had its part to play in the building-up of a pattern. Though the handing over to God of a virginity was a fine and blessed thing, mother-hood must not be depreciated. After all, Julia might become the mother of three sons—three priests. Mrs Dean's prayer might be shaped to some more distant yet even richer fulfilment, such as that. It was not his business to question; but to pray and to trust.

That evening Canon Kirkbride's tiny congregation at Evensong was increased by the addition of Elizabeth Lyte, and after the service she waited for the canon in the church porch. Taken into the rectory study, she very quickly came to the point.

"You know about Howard, Father?"

"I understand that he has gone away."

"To London. The firm has offices there. I think he must have asked to be moved."

"We can assume so," the canon said.

238

Elizabeth produced a letter from her hand-bag. She folded it and handed it to the canon with the clear indication that he should read the one particular half-page.

"You must read that little bit."

The canon found the sentences intended for him.

"Tell Canon Kirkbride that I have a lot to thank him for. I shall write to him personally when I have sorted myself out. Meantime I'd like him to know that we were *not*, after all, wasting our time!"

"I thought I ought to show you it," Elizabeth said, "because it seems to refer to something special between you."

"Yes." The canon gave back the letter. "It does. I'm glad you brought it."

There was a pause. The canon scarcely knew what to say. How did things stand between Elizabeth and Howard? He had no inkling.

Elizabeth saw his uncertainty.

"There is nothing," she said quietly. "It was all a mistake really. I can see now that we were not really suited to each other."

The canon nodded in sympathy.

"But . . ."

Elizabeth broke off abruptly. The canon waited quietly.

"I've been thinking a lot," Elizabeth said. "Everything seems so different now. I don't know how to put it. But it's as though this had to happen just to show me the kind of person I am."

"We can always learn something from these experiences," the canon agreed.

"I learned that I wasn't really in love with Howard. I couldn't have been. At least, not enough to marry him. You see, Father—you'll say this sounds silly—but I was never *desperate* about it."

"We must be thankful that you weren't, in view of what transpired."

Elizabeth's eyes roamed the walls restlessly; the books, the mantelpiece, the statue of Our Lady, the photographs of a soldier in uniform, a cowled and cassocked monk, a mitred bishop. How could she express the inexpressible?

"It isn't that," she said. "But I *needed* to be desperate; if not about that—if not about Howard—then about something else. You said yourself, Father, that I was looking for an opportunity to martyr myself. Do you remember?"

The canon remembered. But he couldn't quite see where all this was drifting.

"This is what I think now," Elizabeth said, more decisively. "Perhaps I'm not the kind of person who does fall in love and marry and have children. Perhaps I'm too restless and unstable. You have to have a kind of poise; you have to be deep and calm to bring up a family—like my mother."

"There is a lot to be said for tranquillity in a mother," the canon agreed, still seeking a glimmer of light.

"And may be," Elizabeth drifted into a half-musing tone again, "I'm not the person to go on typing letters and answering the phone and keeping the manager's engagement book."

240

"You like your work, don't you, Elizabeth?" the canon asked tentatively.

"Father, that's what I've come to see you about. All that typing and listening isn't important enough. And if I'm not the person to become a wife and a mother, well then I must do *something*. I'm not sure what. That's why I've come to ask you. But it must be something definite and big that I can really be keen about. Nursing, welfare work, being with the handicapped—all kinds of thing come to mind. I'd be ready to train; to leave home and join something organized to help people."

"My dear Elizabeth," the canon said, with a smile of profound delight. "It's very good to hear you say so. I shall be only too happy to give you all the help I can. You were quite right to come."

"Well," said Elizabeth, breaking into a smile. "It was you who set me thinking like this."

"Did I?"

The canon's eyes were wide with genuine surprise.

"Yes. What you said, on top of everything that happened. It has all made me feel that you were right. I've got to give myself. Perhaps I've discovered—Oh dear," Elizabeth said, interrupting herself, "it sounds so pompous."

"Perhaps you've discovered a vocation," the canon suggested, completing her sentence.

"Yes," said Elizabeth, "that's what I meant."